Sweetbay Review

Anthology of Southern Virginia

A Writers Studio Publication
A Prize Books Publication

Table of Contents

FICTION

NONFICTION

ABOUT THE AUTHORS

INTRODUCTION

In September of 2005, the Writers Studio held its first meeting. The hope in starting such an organization was that the writers of Southern Virginia would be supported and encouraged in their own personal projects. Monthly meetings, group feedback, discussions on the writing process, guest speakers offering publishing advice, and a monthly newsletter have all been generated toward this end. There was also a plan to create a public venue for the works produced by these writers, and with the publication of our first anthology, we have accomplished this goal.

We hope that you will enjoy the poems, stories, and nonfiction pieces included in these pages. They have been lovingly crafted and presented. If you would like to find out more about the authors, please be sure to glance at the biographies included at the end of the collection.

We would also like to thank Dianne Hills for allowing us to use her painting, *Country Walk*, for the frontispiece and Elizabeth Lovell for designing the cover. Their work was invaluable in the completion of this project.

For more information on the Writers Studio, please email us at: inkwrit@yahoo.com, or visit our website: website: *http://members.gcronline.com/writersstudio/*

POETRY

Thank You, Mr. Hawthorne

by Andy Coe

I should now admit:
From the moment she embroidered,
    and in so doing embraced
    her Letter
— you had me.
I marveled that she
could take what was to be
her shame
    and make it theirs.

Sure, I could not admit it then,
Then, it was drudgery
    of the highest order.
I said I fell asleep reading it,
    and I did.
But what I did not say,
    was that while I slept,
    I dreamed of Pearl.

For skewering hypocrisy;
For speaking to the beauty
    of bearing suffering with dignity;
For inviting not only your epoch to the mirror,
— but my own,
even though it lay some two hundred
years hence from yours;

Thank you.

I should tell you now:
I wish I could have taken Hester
to my prom.

Self Indulgence for Breakfast

by Andy Coe

6:27 am
Sounds of shattering glass
and wrenching steel
exhume me.

I don't peer out
my window to see
if everyone is ok.

Instead I resent the
breaching of my repose.
I was not planning to
start my wound-licking
for another hour-and-a-half
at least.

No chance of going back to sleep
Not in a room this cold.
How long to lie here in
my stale space
before straggling to my kitchen…

Where, rather than making breakfast,
I resent the pile of dirty dishes in the sink.
Then, I sit down and write a self-indulgent poem.

It was titled, "A Bad Dream."

The first line was "6:27 am"

Now, some twelve years hence,
I have stumbled across it in an old notebook,
and I am embarrassed.
— heartbreak seduces you into thinking

self-absorption is comforting.

Embarrassed, not at how bad the poem was,
— and it was awful,
but about the fact that I forgot about
the people in the car
entirely.

I never even looked.

The Locksmith

by Andy Coe

She is in a room
That locks from the Inside
Alone with her demons

> *What's that noise*
> *Someone's coming*
> *Oh my God...*

And all I can do
Is to bore a peep hole.
I am here for her
But she is there
And so we remain
Both alone

> *There's a hole in the door*
> *Someone is here*
> *Thank God I'm not alone*
> *It's been so long...*

So I can see her eye
Straining through my gift portal
And she can appreciate my presence

> *But he is still there*
> *And I am stuck in here*

Still alone, really

Except when it reminds her
That I am here for her,
But she is still there
In the room
That locks from the inside

Just keep looking out
Don't turn around
What was that?
Don't
turn
around
"Thank you for being there for me"

The eyes are the windows
to the soul
The windows with no shades
no blinds
But the door has a lock
that locks
from the Inside.

That it's enough to know someone is there
is a very comforting lie

We both know

what she does not say –

she believes even more:

that the demons she won't look at

but still sees

hold her Key.

And I am wondering

if the peep hole is the kindness I intended

or a cruel irony.

Maybe I should extend

my finger –

poke her in the eye

What if that caused her

to turn around

and appear to the demons

to be winking at them –

> *What's this*
> *in my pocket…*

Demons hate being winked at

— would that put them on their heels

and give her the edge she needs

in her fight

in her room

that locks

from the Inside.

> *…A key*

A Gentle Nature

by Barbara Hatcher Shaver

Where should I go; what should I do?
Tell me now as you did before
when life was young and
the trees were budding.

Tell me now as you did before.
Be gentle, loving, and kind.
The trees were budding;
not changing and distilled.

Be gentle, loving, and kind.
This, I can handle;
not changing and distilled
as fading grass turns into straw.

This, I can handle.
Oceans roll and the sun sets.
As fading grass turns into straw,
no one fully understands His gentle nature.

A Day in Time

by AVE el

Swaying palms flash over the golden ball

Rising

Leaves clap their hands

Today go for a run in the warm white sand

Stopping to dabble in the water

Oh, pain awaits,

Careless or forgetful sunbathers

Wandered aimlessly "who cares"

They say

Left clutter along the bay

Now walk I must.

Excitement mounts as tiny pebbles

And shells shine

Fascinated no two alike

Each is examined and stowed away

Time elapsed

Near sunset ardent runners pound

Along the manmade dike

Delicious aromas hang heavily

In the air

Indulge in a cozy spot

Savor a smooth rich filling éclair

To think out clearly

Life's sorted plot

Intensely pondering all that summer

Has in store

Simple and meaningless things

Satisfying to some, yet
To others a bore
Ashen planks shade runners
Oh, the exhilarating sun
A tiny part
A DAY IN TIME brings.

The Stillness

by AVE el

A lone whippoorwill
echoes triumphantly in
the night
a restless sick child
tosses violently
grasping for life
Suddenly a stillness
Enters—
tearful mother
quiet your anxious
desperation
come dawn's glorious
light
your son
will win
the fight.

The Glow

by AVE el

The golden sky is cracking.

A glowing ball

Shines through slivers of

Bright topaz

Drifting away to nothing

To become

Tomorrow's sunrise.

Unwind

by Doris Ragland

Let us stop the constant grind
Take time out to unwind.
Slow the thought and clear the mind,
Stop the clock and forget the time.

Enjoy the ripple of the sea,
And listen to the crickets plea.
Rest the muscles relax the nerves
Be ready for action when it's time to serve.

It's so good to be full of life,
But at the end we pay a price,
If we keep working over time,
And never stop to unwind.

Naturalized

by Don Conner

On the coldest of winter days,
he was naturalized.
Against a dull December sky,
he waxed one of us;
unshackled his island childhood
of coconuts and want.
Raised a right palm with scars,
aimed patriotic monosyllables
at a legal man,
himself becoming legal in the process.
Smiled at the crowd, broke bread,
as his heart pumped red
(white and blue) beneath the little flag
pinned to his chest by an Army nurse
that he would later know as Sue;
meet, melt, woo,
marry and die beside;
by then a citizen, a senator, a saint—
beneath flesh-colored paint.

Piedmont Farmgirl

by Don Conner

The dog, recently puppied,

    with teats dangling

    peers cautiously around the porch.

An old washtub

    tumescent with rainwater

    guards the corner of the house.

A chair, without a back

    sits disconsolately

    in the yard—it is

Fronted by packed earth,

    grass worn away

    by the shuffling of hungry feet.

Feet that rebel at sitting,

    while the stomach gnaws,

    urging pursuit of bread.

The wind blows

    and creaks New Deal hinges

    on the weatherbeaten door.

A thin girl emerges from within,

    walks into the rain

without a raincoat.

Her destination plain
    against the sky
    of grey—she smiles,

Then off to church
    for promises
    of a better day.

Drugstore Poet

by Don Conner

petty phrases, pretty,
but hollow lines,
hardbound to sell better.

he who
rode a subway,
saw a star
touched a young girl:
all experiences of
his aesthetic world.

Milton and Eliot, I wept,
your covenants, falsely kept,

cuddle beside the freshman's pillow,
color her dreams,
on the cover of a magazine
go to Russia next spring—
cultural exchange.

speech, speech, the masses clamor
for their latest literary glamour.
behind the lectern, lights shove . . .
he writes of love
on a bus
in the park

after dark

beneath a sweater.
hardbound to sell better.

he is well read—
by waifs in truck stops,
faces in beauty shops,
teenage teardrops.
and—poetic injustice—
gets by with it all!
is invited to a ball
where ladies in collars
beg charity's dollar.

his verse through their
sewing circles sifted,
they come away murmuring—
he is gifted! he is gifted!

Winter Wonderland

by Ruthann P. Anderson

The frozen earth turned to white
On a cold and blustery night.
The trees and ground were dressed in glitter.
This was a gift from Ole Man Winter.
Snow fell throughout the next day
Showing where wildlife came out to play.
Footprints large and small were seen
In the snow so white and clean.
It was fun to see who went where
And learn more about wildlife living there.

Standing Proud and Tall

by Ruthann P. Anderson

The old wooden house burned to the ground;
Ashes and burnt timbers lay all around.
But the stone chimney stood proud and tall.
It did not waiver; it did not fall.
It's a sad sight to see;
There was little left of what used to be.

Thick

by Margaret S. Covington

Thick

Thick's high density, bubbly blue ooze fills a clear test tube.

The saturated glob smothers movement.

Thick's oozy blob radiates sparkling light and emits the pure scent of freshly washed towels.

Wet granules of laundry detergent cannot plop from the upside down test tube.

Thick is constipating.

Dig thick out with your latex covered index finger...

Is thick useful?

Thick

Thick's stately pillars support the opulent, historical monuments laden with high moral values.

The cool, gray, massive walls protect us from occasional clashes with time and nature.

Thick's stable foundation never intends to desert us and lays hidden below, constantly supportive.

Thick is comforting.

Press your face upon the shaded marble walls...

Is thick absorbent?

Thick

Thick's beautifully wrapped packaged vacations are surprises from out of the blue.

Luscious verbiage flatters you, expecting that you will like her.

It is not tricky, really. However, "thick" can lead you to jump to erroneous conclusions.

Thick is stupidity.

Take your time and open your perfect package with nimble, well manicured

fingers...

Is thick "simply" exposed?

Thick

Thick's sweet maple syrup saturates a buttered morning pancake, a syrupy sponge.

The savory concentration craves pleasure, eternal ecstasy.

Thick doesn't eradicate your deepest urges, it merely summons them.

Thick is desirous.

Pull this succulent paradise through your teeth and paste your palate dozens upon

dozens of times...

Is thick satisfied?

Thick is nothing new, yet it blocks us or serves as protection

It condenses what we know, possibly making room to learn more.

There is nothing fragile about thick.

There is nothing creative about thick; we just keep piling on more "thick" into

thicker mounds.

What a shame

Thick is just thick

Or is it?

I Loved You at "Hello"

by Mabel Janet Wood

When we met I was alone
not lonely

Our eyes met
then danced a flirtation dance
Yours pierced me

We chatted moments of nothingness
Slowly carefully
getting to know each other

Your kiss
was like a warm bayou breeze
You consumed me with your essence

I loved you at "Hello"

Mountains in the Fall

by Mabel Janet Wood

Like paint on a canvas moving left to right,
    The tapestry on the slopes is a brilliant sight.
With hues that range from red to gold,
    Some colors are dull, while others are bold.
The changing of the colors is quite unique,
    From mid-thru-late October, the beauty's at its peak.
If you yell to the slopes, an echo will call,
    "I'll always want to visit the MOUNTAINS IN THE FALL."

The Womb

by Shirley A. Mandel

I live in a worldly womb
   with many parts being shaped
in the shades and shadows of the earth.

Eyes are being formed that
  have seen the shades of the day.
I have seen the shadow of a man
   who preached the Word on Sunday,
and I have seen a diamond shine
      in the shadow of a starless night.

My heart is being shaped
  by the many colors of the world.
The soft yellows and greens of the Earth
    have given me a generous heart
while the steely blues of loss and poverty
have made me compassionate toward friends.

Arms are being formed in the fullness
  of the sun
that can hold a hurting friend to my breast
like God held me when I was stricken
    and in a prison for the sick.

Knees are being formed when I pray
while light and darkness crisscross my bed.

Hands and fingers are being formed
    in white shadows for service
because I have found hope
    in the many works of Jesus Christ.

    Soon
my fingers shall serve a breathing Christ
      when I am born
        with much pain
          from this womb
     into the kingdom of God.

The Stigma of Nature

by Shirley A. Mandel

Above the trees
   gleams a sea of blue space
      rimmed with gold.
It's the sky,
the still waters of doves and eagles.
But often,
  when the gold is marred
    by the dust of an angry cloud,
and the still waters are rent by a rage,
the sky becomes
    the birth-mother of destruction.
For all the hostile
   forces of nature
meet to war there.

Beneath the trees
  little flowers grow
   by rotting stumps and logs.
In the fall the trees
  share their ginger with the ground,
but venomous snakes,
  also the color of ginger,
    live among the leaves.

In a tree
  a bird carefully weaves

a hollow home for her progeny.

She will nurture her eggs
   to be the mirror image of herself
      and her mate,
until her glorious children take wing.
But soon the Earth will tilt
   the other way,
and her empty home
     will turn a frosty, winter gray.

Finally
between the trees
   there stands a man,
as bright as the corona of the morning,
     with flowers in his hand.
But deep,
in the darker soils of his inner earth,
there grows a thistle.
  In richer soils, he nurtures sin.

Perpetual Safety

by Shirley A. Mandel

The eye of the storm was red
    and glowering
like the eye of a man's
singed with anger.
Images of dust and rubble
    were forming in my mind
because the wrath of nature
    was about to fall on us.
I lay on my stomach
    to protect my face against the storm.
It was then I heard
    the rustle of a soft robe,
and I felt Him whisper
    into my soul;
be at peace my friend
in me is perpetual safety.

On Your Wedding Day

by Michele Marko Fitch

On your wedding day did you imagine....

Happy days to come?

Was your mind full of hope for the future? Or did you just soak up the exciting feelings of the present day?

Did you think about children and grandchildren and how they would turn out?

Did you imagine gymnastic programs, dance recitals, band and chorus concerts?

Did you see yourself as a scout leader or volunteer?

Did you imagine exciting vacations and traveling to all fifty states?

Did you think that pizza could actually taste like cardboard?

Did you think that you would acquire so many nursing skills?

Were your thoughts only hopeful? Or did you have some fears?

Or were you confident in knowing any sadness could be overcome together?

No, some things that have happened you could have never imagined.

And some things you imagined may not have come true (at least not yet).

You have faced the unexpected both good and bad with strength, calmness and resilience. A true example to everyone around you.

And as you now look back on everything that has happened,

focus on the smiles and not the tears.

Celebrate the victories and know that the defeats have made you stronger.

40 years, what a celebration!

Happy Anniversary!

Love,

Michele

Jolly Mr. Holly

by Lillian K. Stumm and Michele Marko Fitch

'Twas Christmas Eve and all was still—the big round moon was mellow.
I want to tell you a story about a funny fellow.
I took a penny that was bright and shiny new,
And laid it just outside our door to see what it would do.

I sat, watched, listened and waited but soon I fell fast asleep.
I'd grown so tired of waiting that my watch I could not keep.
But suddenly I heard a sound of twinkling bells a-ringing.
I listened very carefully; then I heard somebody singing.

I looked out of the window and I saw to my surprise,
A very funny fellow—he was just about my size.
He had a snowball body and a little snowball head,
And dark eyes that twinkled and a candy nose so red.

He wore a tall black stovepipe hat and showing underneath,
Was holly hair that curled around and made a pretty wreath.
His mouth was almost hidden by a mistletoe mustache,
And around his body was a wide red cotton sash.
For buttons he had jingle bells and as he skipped along,
They tinkle twinkled merrily and played a happy song.

He swung his little candy cane just like drum majors do.
He twirled it and spun it a-round then in the air it flew.
He never failed to catch it as it came a-spinning down.
And then he took a tumble like a funny circus clown.

Just then he spied the penny lying right beside our door.
And as he stooped to pick it up, He jingled even more.
Now bending down is quite a job for anyone so fat.
I thought he'd topple over—or maybe lose his hat.
He reached into his pocket, and he drew out something white.
He laid it down beside the door then vanished out of sight.

Although I could not see him, I heard him clearly say:
"I hope that you will have a very happy Christmas Day!"
I quickly opened up the door and ran outside to see,
Just what it was this funny fellow kindly left for me.

I found a big white envelope and when I looked inside,
I found a lovely card which said "A Happy Christmas Tide."
And at the bottom it was signed in letters big and clear:
From Jolly Mr. Holly—Have a Happy Brand New Year.

I also found so many candy canes. It was more than I could eat.
Who'd think for just a penny, you would get so fine a treat.
I went inside and went to bed as happy as could be.
To think that Mr. Holly made a visit here to me.

Next day I told my mother of the visit and she said,
"I think you had too many tarts before you went to bed."
"But mother 'twas no dream," I cried, "Here's proof as you can see.
These candy canes and Christmas card he really left for me."

There are many more candy canes than I could ever eat.

I will give one away to every one I meet.

For Jolly Mr. Holly showed me how happy he could be

When he gave me such a special gift and saw my face light up with glee.

Now some folks say I dreamed it all and if you think so too,

Next Christmas lay a penny out—you'll see what it will do.

Big Top

by Melissa Elmes

i.

When you were two, we went to the circus.

It was one of those one-ring Big Tops
(the kind you won't find anymore in five years' time.)

The canvas tent was striped blue-and-white, and
dappled with spots of sunlight through
so many holes that it was a good thing
it wasn't raining.

For two hours, your free admission and my twenty dollars
paid for our spots in that hot, torn tent.

I considered that money well spent,
watching you watch the elephants.

ii.

At the circus,
there was a beautiful, dark-haired woman
wearing white spangles and flesh-colored tights.

I watched you watch in awe

as she swung back-and-forth
high above our seats
on the trapeze.

If she had swung closer,
we might have seen
the mended seams and stains
on her once-pristine costume.

But as I watched you watch her,
I was glad you were only two
and that didn't matter to you.

iii.

It was a small, one-ring Big Top,
and everyone pulled double-duty:
The Ringmaster cued the piped-in music, and
Gabriella, the Flying Wonder from Brazil,
took your picture with the monkey during intermission.

We watched Max, the Hungarian tightrope walker,
and I noticed that Max bore a striking resemblance
to the brother in the Argentinian brother-sister team
that earlier awed the crowd on the Rolabola.

As I watched the five dollar Polaroid take shape,
you watched the horse-and-pony act in the ring below,

not caring that they were the same ones
giving three dollar rides outside before the show.

I was glad that you were two years old at the circus, that day.

iv.

There weren't any tigers at the circus,
but there were two horses and two elephants.
There was a python to take pictures with,
and a monkey wearing a costume, who
made faces at the camera and cooed at you.

There was a little dog, too - a toy poodle, who
cavorted around the ring with a clown, the dog
dressed up in a tiny horse costume,
pulling double-duty with the rest of them.

All the animals looked healthy and well-fed
and the crowd was pleased with their performances.
You laughed and laughed when the little horse
trotted in figure-eights around the big horse's legs.

I watched you laughing, and thought about our three dogs at home,
who curl up next to you when you sleep.
I hope that at the end of the day, the poodle-pony
curls up cozily with his proud clown handler.

v.

The circus came to town
"For two days only!"
And we all flocked to see the sights.

I spent more time watching you
laughing and staring in wonder
than I did watching the show.

Perhaps that is why I was surprised
when the show came to an end and, looking up,
I found that with expert swiftness
the roadies had already dismantled half the Big Top from
around our heads.

Tomorrow, this one-ring Big Top will be assembled somewhere else;
in five years, it might never be set up again anywhere at all.
I hope another two year old laughs and stares in wonder first.

the lightness of being

by s.m. foran

i watch the softened whiteness of her legs
hesitant in the shadowed twilight
see the hands cup together, release
come together once again

she forgets that i am watching
intent on scooping curled palms
back and forth through midsummer air
and softly caging the brilliance of fireflies

these gently pulsing luminaries glide past
somehow sensing innocence
in the unpracticed movements of one unused to chasing stars
and for a moment pause

their flight of fancy interrupted
an episodic surrender of the divine

FICTION

The Time Machine Epilogue

Fan Fiction of the Public Domain H. G. Wells

Novel, *The Time Machine*

by Susan Hall Jernigan

I have been a faithful friend and servant to the Time Traveler, as I refer to him now, as it has been seven years since he was last seen or heard from. I have visited his residence every year on the anniversary of his story of the Morlocks and Elois. I am hoping to find some kind of sign that he has made it back in future to save Weena from the Morlocks. Being the practical person that I am, it is best that I have him declared legally dead, so family and friends can move on, myself included. I, on the other hand, believe that he is still alive and living with Weena in the very, very distant future. I let his housekeeper, Miss Watchit move on. She has gone to live with the very young man and his wife; they having a handful of children of various ages, needed some help. She says it is only until the Time Traveler returns, and I am to let her know immediately upon his return.

It is with dread that I opened the door to his laboratory, as I have done on this day every year for the past seven years, only to find that he had not come back and that my trip had only made me more certain of his future. Things seemed to be different this time, but I could not make out the changes. Some things seemed to be missing, and the dust seemed to hold footprints that are not mine. The strange floral scent that filled the air seemed to be coming from the flowers that were now in the vase by the window, and a letter was propped up in front, there in the Time Traveler's handwriting, my name in bold letters. My heart soared. I know now that he had been here, and I had not missed him by much, because the flowers seemed to have been just cut. Not knowing what to do, at first, I sat down for my legs were weak with the idea that he had been here. I hesitated at the thought of opening his letter; my hands were shaking with excitement. I carefully opened the letter and started to read with a joy that had captured my heart. I let out the breath that I did not know I was holding.

Dear Sir,

I hope this letter finds you in good health and spirits, as I am happier than I have ever been.

Let me start from the beginning, actually from where I left off, with the story of the Morlocks and the Elois. I realize that if the human race was to continue I had to go forward and change the way things were heading. The Elois could no longer go on being food for the Morlocks, and the prospect of the world being inhabited by giant crabs was just something I could not live with, as I despise the little critters. From the enclosed photograph you can be certain that I made it back in time to save Weena from the Morlocks, and the child with us is none other than our son, and soon we will be blessed with another child. Being that you are the practical man that I know you to be, you have or are now declaring me dead, even as you are reading this, but know that I am very much alive. The thought of coming back has crossed my mind, but being the scientist that I am, I could not take the chance that Weena and our children would make the trip back in time, being that they are only alive in this time. I could not risk losing them for they are my life. I have often thought of you and the others and wonder if I ever cross your minds, know that I tell the story of my trip back and the shocked looks on all your faces of how my story left many of you speechless, about what the future holds, but know that I have changed the outcome, and the Morlocks are no more. It is with a heavy heart that I must tell you that I will not be coming back, and I would like for you to sell my home and invest the money in the education of the young, for they are indeed our future.

There in the Time Traveler's bold handwriting his name and the date of today. I looked at the photograph of the Time Traveler and the pretty blonde woman heavy with child, at his side, and the small boy so like the Time Traveler with the same gray eyes and pale face. I wiped at the tears that had freely fallen from my eyes and folded the letter ever so carefully and replaced it in the envelope, along with the photograph, of which it came and gently placed it in my pocket over my heart. I knew now that my yearly trips to the Time Traveler's laboratory had not been in vain, and I could rest now knowing that he is happy and he is were he was meant to be. Now I can start living the rest of my life, not worrying about what tomorrow brings.

Just in Case

by Gene Curtis

The four-year-old boy screamed at the top of his lungs. "I want some soda!"

The lady I took to be his mother looked toward the ceiling of the small theater and shook her head. She was rather young, I thought, to be a mother of such a thing, but I remembered, once upon a time, I used to be such a thing myself. At four years old, nothing exists in the world save what you perceive to affect you, and at that age not much affects you for very long. Right now there was only one thing he observed to be affecting him, and he wasn't shy about vocalizing it. That needed to change. The movie would start in a few minutes, and this kid needed something to occupy his petite imagination.

She picked up her drink and offered to let him sip from the straw.

He screamed, "Is it cola or soda?"

"It's soda, orange soda."

A mild sigh of disgust oozed from the crowd of movie goers.

"It's pop, kid… at least that's what they used to call it… well, until too many people started losing their noses or dying," I said.

The kid turned in his seat, getting to his knees to look at who had dared speak to him. I turned my attention to the mother. "Folks call me Carolina Jones, ma'am. I might be of some assistance."

She shrugged. "If you think it'll help."

I nodded once and looked back at the kid. "I used to work for the government… a long time ago. I had an interesting job. You see, I had to catalogue all of the rare and dangerous animals in North America. I was kind of like that crocodile guy you see on television. You know the one I mean, don't you? The one that's always jumping around, squatting and saying 'Crimey.'"

The kid hunched down a bit so just his eyes and the top of his head showed over the back of the seat.

"Do you know why he's always doing that? Well, crimey is an Australian word that means 'I just soiled my britches.' You know what that is, don't you?"

The kid held up two fingers.

"He won't come up around these parts 'cause he's scared. He's read my book about rare wild animals, and he don't want nothing to do with the saber tooth grindleback. Can't say I blame him, though. If I didn't know the secret, I can't say that I would stay around these parts myself.

"Folks used to call all soft drinks," I leaned in close to the lad, cupped my hands around my mouth and whispered, "soda pop, or just pop for short." I sat back in my seat and continued. "But that sounds an awful lot like the male grindleback's aggression call, the sound he makes just before he attacks. Now, when a grindleback hears that call, he knows he's about to be attacked so he attacks first.

"Now, a grindleback has an interesting method of attack. Its teeth are sharper than a samurai sword, and it's fearsome quick. It usually goes for the nose first, especially if it wants you to drop what you have, like a grape soda. They really like grape sodas. If you don't drop the soda, or if you don't have any left, especially if you have any on your breath, it'll tear your head clean off and climb down your throat to get at it.

"To complicate matters, you don't ever know where they're hiding. They love to hide under things in dark places, like in the woods, garbage dumps, and just about anywhere they can get under something in the dark."

The theater lights began fading, and the kid's eyes widened.

"There's only one thing that the grindleback likes to drink more than grape soda... orange soda. And, there is only one thing... one thing only, that can keep a grindleback from attacking. I'm the only one that knows what that one thing is. I always keep at least one with me at all times. It's my secret. I never put it in the book, and that crocodile fellow doesn't know about it. That's why he's too scared to come to these parts. He wrote me one time and asked about it, but I won't tell him."

I reached into my shirt pocket, withdrew a movie theater sized stick of chocolate flavored caramel and held it in front of his eyes. "You see, the saber tooth grindleback loves to *eat* fresh caramel more than anything else. The right kind of caramel gets stuck in its teeth and annoys it so much it can't attack for at least ten seconds. That gives you just enough time to set your soda down and back away very slowly. Once you're far enough away, you can cut out and head for the hills, so to speak." I shook the piece of candy at him and said, "You take this one, just in case. You have orange soda on your breath. I have another one, and I'm drinking a cola. Just make sure you keep the wrapper on it so it stays fresh… just in case."

The kid stayed quiet, occasionally glancing around at the empty chairs nearby, all-the-while clutching that piece of candy. After the movie he turned around and asked, "Are you from North Carolina?"

I stood and put my hat on. "Yep, but my dad was from Indiana. He taught me to be prepared… just in case." I winked and patted my pocket.

Excerpts from *Regal Wind*

by Gene Curtis

Regal Wind *is a Young Adult Action-Adventure novel set in the present turmoil of religious fanaticism and terrorist activities. The young hero, Jeanne Wilcox, discovers a terrorist action designed to hijack the cruise ship Regal Wind just after the ship is underway. The terrorists have piloted a huge radioactive bomb, essentially a small submarine filled with explosives and radioactive material, under the cruise ship and attached it to the hull. While leaving U.S. waters, the cruise ship sails through a thunderstorm and is struck by lightning which, in combination with the radioactivity, sends the cruise ship back in time to the year 600 A.D. to a location off the coast of Spain in the Mediterranean Sea. The ship is boarded by Visigoth raiders, and the expected mayhem ensues. After this battle is over, the fleet of the Visigoth king, commanded by Claude the Noble, approaches and attempts to board the ship by trick. Regal Wind's captain, Bjorn Koenraad tries to pacify Claude the Noble with his version of an Irish blessing. The other character in this part of the story is the ship's first officer, Tic.*

The last part of the epilogue chapter is an epic story-poem that tells of this encounter from a Visigoth sailor's point of view.

Regal Wind's Bridge
8:31 am

Jeanne knocked on the door to the bridge and was greeted by Tic holding a pistol.

"Sorry, Jeanne, we're playing it safe."

"I kind of expected that. Listen, I need to collect some water samples away from the ship. Any ideas on how I can do that?"

"Do you dive?"

"Sure, got my card when I was twelve."

"If the captain says okay, then I'll go with you. Come on in."

Tic turned to face the captain. "Sir, Miss Wilcox has requested that she be allowed to collect some water samples away from the ship."

Captain Koenraad looked toward Jeanne. "Water samples?"

"Yes, sir, I'm still trying to figure out what's going on."

"You can do that after we clear these vessels that are approaching. I understand you're a pretty good linguist. Would you mind accompanying me to hail them and see if they can tell us where we are?"

Jeanne looked out the windows and saw that the approaching ships were close. "I'd be glad to."

"Well, then, shall we go. I could use a nice sea breeze on my face."

"One thing, Captain, if we're going to let these ships get close, then it might be a good idea to warn people to stay inside. We don't know if they're hostile, the first ones were."

He looked at her and smiled. "Better to err on the side of prudence." He walked over to the island console, flipped a switch and leaned to the mike.

"Ladies, gentlemen and crew, this is the captain. There are several ships approaching, and we have no idea of their intent. For your safety, please remain off the outside decks until that can be determined."

* * *

All of the ships furled their sails about a hundred yards off the port bow. Jeanne and the captain watched from the narrow deck on level five. One ship sprouted oars and started approaching with the oars swinging to the sound of a slow, hollow drum beat. They stopped about twenty yards abeam. Shields picketed the galleon's port gunwale.

Captain Koenraad shouted, "Ahoy."

A single figure stood toward the bow of the ship, bracing his shield to his torso with his left arm and holding a short sword in his right hand. His helmet was unadorned. He called, "Oy," and followed that with a short phrase that Jeanne took to be related to low German.

"I can't be absolutely sure, but I think he just asked the name of the god of this ship and said his name is Claude the Noble Goth."

Captain Koenraad chuckled, "That's the first time I've been called a god. Tell him Bjorn Koenraad commands this ship."

Jeanne relayed the information, and the fellow said, "Coin Red," and followed with another question.

"Sir, I think he wants to know what tribute the god Koenraad wishes so he'll leave this sea."

"Tribute? Who's he kidding? Ask him where we are."

Jeanne asked, and the response was, "Corse', Sardegna," followed by pointing his sword east. He asked again, "What tribute?"

"I caught that, Corsica, Sardinia that way," and he pointed east.

"Captain, he still asks what tribute."

"Tell him thanks, no tribute, we're leaving."

She relayed the information, and the guy raised his sword and yelled.

"Sir, he says you humiliate him by making him ask thrice 'What tribute to leave this sea.' I might have it wrong. He might be asking you to bless this sea."

"Tell him, may your sails be filled always and may your nets be overflowing, may your enemies bow at your feet and may the riches of the earth be yours."

She did. "Captain, he says a blessing is a curse without tribute, and he will not ask again."

The man brought his sword down hard, and a flight of arrows launched from between the shields.

Jeanne yelled, "Duck!" and pushed the captain behind a steel I-beam that spanned from floor to ceiling against the wall.

The arrows bounced off the wall and clattered to the floor. Another flight launched, and the other ships began hoisting sail.

Jeanne said, "We're sitting ducks here. After the next shot, make a run for the door."

The arrows tinged off the walls again, and they broke for the door. They reached the door, and the next flight of arrows landed. Captain Koenraad took one in the back of his left shoulder. He hurried to the nearby phone attached to the wall just inside the casino.

"Tic, get this tub underway! Full speed straight ahead!"

Two seconds later the ship lurched forward, and all the galleons started closing in.

Captain Koenraad looked out the door. "What the hell! They're using ballista."

Jeanne looked out. The three lead ships were rigged with ballista fore and aft like harpoons, firing bolts attached to lines. Three had already fired, and they were coming about to fire the aft launchers. They were falling away and would have to fire the next volley in a hurry, even if it was futile against the steel hull of the ship.

The Regal Wind reached speed, and the fleet of galleons had no hope of catching a ship traveling at seven times their maximum.

Jeanne said, "Captain, let's get you to the doctor."

He said, "Yes, let's do that. It looks like I finally got the point."

Epilogue
Six Months Later

Jeanne picked through the stack of mail and found a large envelope from Captain Koenraad. She opened it and began reading:

Jeanne Wilcox
901 Broad Leaf Trail
Hanover, MD 21076

Dear Jeanne,
    I know you'll find what I've enclosed very interesting. I made a copy for you just after I read it.
    Be sure to keep me informed about how your dad is doing.
Until we meet again,

Capt. Bjorn

enclosure

From the Desk of Dr. W. H. Brickell

Captain Bjorn Koenraad
1219 Great Ship Quay
Fort Lauderdale, FL 33316

Dear Captain Koenraad,

    I read with great interest the recent news media reports concerning you and your ship's recent exploits involving temporal shifting. I think you will find equally interesting the enclosed copy of the translation of a document I worked on some years back.

    The original document was recovered in a rare find of the Visigoth King Liuva II's (circa 601 A.D – 603 A.D.) scarce official writings. I had initially believed this to be a fanciful tale told to the king for his amusement and that he had liked it well enough to record it. I have recently revised that assessment. (King Liuva II was the son of King Reccared, mentioned in the story, (circa 581 A.D.- 601 A.D.) and succeeded him to the throne.)

    Please note that the story is incomplete as the parchment it was recorded on was moderately fragmented, with portions sufficiently decayed to be unintelligible and in some places entirely missing. In translating the story, I tried to maintain the sense of meter and rhyme where possible, but a lot of the nuance was lost in the translation. Of note, the name "Coin Red" is a transliteration, as I originally thought it was a better fit than copper and/or pence or penny. I am glad to see I was correct in that assumption.

Sincerely,

Wilhelm H. Brickell, PhD
Institute for Archaic Studies
Stockholm, Sweden

enclosure

I Alone

Of gods or devils, titans or mortals

I know not, for none could tell.

What came to pass still baffles,

But I alone have survived to tell the tale.

There came upon the sea a great tempest.
Fire and thunder, rain and gale.
Of the king's armada five scout ships bore witness.
I alone have returned to tell the tale.

The tempest was over, and gulls did fly.
Upon the horizon a ship so vast.
Ten legions she could hold but
No sails or rigging nor nary a mast.

Of the scout ships one departed,
For the news must be told.
Great riches for the taking:
Weapons and machines, jewels and gold!

By night the four remaining rowed an approach
For great riches the great ship must hold.
We dreamt the life of kings and nobles
And imagined soon our lot would unfold.

The great ship was taller than our highest masts,
So from mast top high with ropes we boarded
Port and starboard, fore and aft…
With ease and quiet, we were not thwarted.

My eyes beheld doors of crystal,
Carpets of Persia, brass of high polish,
Ebony and stained glass, paintings of wonder
Riches beyond measure, so much to relish.

A feast for kings we beheld.

But what be these that none could savor?

Wines of black, red and amber, some hot, some cold.

All strange for there was no smell or flavor.

Men of Arabia in battle we engaged

Few and without armor they came.

Their weapons of thunder ripped and tore

Against such none could tame.

Yet sword and arrow wounded them sore

Valiant they fought on thru the night...

We failed to take the ship

Against their weapons of such might.

Of gods or devils, titans or mortals,

I know not, for none could tell.

And I alone have survived

To tell the tale.

The battle raged on, our many, their few.

Thunder and brimstone, sword and arrow,

Many were slain until we were few.

We were tired to the marrow.

From behind me came great thunder and great force.

By a hand unseen from low, over the side I flew.

Down to the water, plunging in the depths,

There'd be no chance for treasure, this I knew.

I surfaced and saw the great ship begin to move.
No sails, no wind, no oars... she went.
Water is the grave of many.
Yet by fate I'm not yet spent.

Masts lashed of the scout ships four
When the great ship did sail
The ships sloshed and foundered,
Save the masts and top sail

However, all was not kaput.
Afloat by plank I woke drifting
By morn's light I saw billows of sail,
The fleet of **Reccared** the great king.

By trick Claude did plan,
To take the great ship wherein
By tribute and lie he would breach
The great ship to slay all therein

Coin Red, master of the great ship
Hailed from lowest deck Claude the Noble
And questions three he did ask
What course? What land? Why trouble?

Answers three Claude did give,
West! Corsica. To pay thee tribute.
Coin Red refused the tribute thrice,
And to us a curse he did impute.

"The wind will blow your sails,
Your catch will be a heap.
Your enemies will whisper at your feet,
Thus the riches of Earth will you reap."

Claude the Noble would not accept defeat.
Attack! He cried and arrows were shot.
None found purchase on a hull as iron.
Thus we saw his trick come to naught.

Ballista! He commanded
Around we rowed and oars did moan
Three bolts were launched
It was like feathers on stone.

No wind, nor sail the great ship did move
With great force by Neptune's very hand
Faster than a horse like a mountain she went.
To catch her, great speed we could not command.

By oar and sweat to Corsica's shore we returned
Four score warriors of the great ship we did find.
Appearing as men of Arabia but
All strange of garb, of deed and mind.

On the eighth day they did die
And lo, their flesh did not rot
Neither vulture nor fly nor worm nor stench
Of fear none would bury, burn or cart.

Of gods or devils, titans or mortals, I know not,
Yet I say true we were curst.
In days to come the curse I'd see
Our fate and fortune turn to worst.

The East Wind came thru the night
With net and spear we set sail
On return our holds were full
Fish, so, so many we could not sell.

One pence for ten, thus the curse
For Coin Red had spoken thus,
Your catch will be a burden.
Ill fortune we began to cuss.

Once again upon the sea,
A west wind came as a gale
Tales of riches hidden on island shore
A course for Sicily we set sail

Claude sent spies of five, I was one
To scout the people and the land.
Seven days to find legend's treasure
And by stealth deliver to his hand.

Should we fail in this quest
Claude will march by the night
Slaying all by morn's cresting sun
And take the treasure by his might.

By cockcrow of the morrow

Twixt dune and sand I lay hidden.

For there approached a merchant

With horse and goods laden wagon.

I took his clothes and his guise.

As a merchant traveling to the village

I rode there upon horse drawn cart

With dreams of vast loot and pillage.

Travelers passed and spoke not a word

And by midday I came to the square

People here and there, to and fro

I was greeted by a maiden, young and fair

She beckoned "What wares, good sir? For I may trade."

Her words like a dove, soft and low.

In the guise of a merchant I waved

"I pray thee say what I may show."

A pot and cloth she did covet

But coin or jewel she had none

"I came for trade and gain," I bellowed

"But with paupers I am undone."

"Surely good sir, I have worth."

She bowed and with eyes most kind

Bid me to the ground.

What worth did she have in mind?

"Good sir a slave I'm not
Nor do I play the wench
But I might repair your coat
Or yon harness' torn cinch"

I nodded then grinned.
"Then, a story I'll have of Goths of old.
I'll trade either not both, the pot or cloth
For a tale of daring and gold."

She smiled and bowed once more.
She thought a moment with a frown
She cast her gaze here and there
She began to speak and looked back down.

"Long years have past since Goths did rule
Across the land with pillage and plunder.
Rome's fair riches the hordes amassed
And hid in a great cave down under"

She knew not where this cave may be
Nor what riches lie in store.
The story came from her mother
Who told her tales of yore.

Six days more I searched the land.
No sign, no clue, I found but dust
The day would dawn with Claude the Noble
Slaying all by slashing and thrust

But by morn's light upon yonder mount
Claude the Noble I did see.
Sword, arrow and lance
His legion divided in three.

He called, "Fair people of this good land
Lost treasure I've come to reap.
Seek not courage to make a stand
But render unto me what I seek."

A village council was called in haste
All to come to the market square.
After quick words it was agreed
Yield the cache, and do not err.

Thus came to pass as Coin Red had spoke
"The people will whisper at your feet."
Claude the Noble was led to the cave
From his prize they planned to cheat.

Parties four entered with torch
By eve they returned with what they'd found.
Jewel and gold as legend had said
There was too much, enough to astound.

Unseen, unheard, unknown men went
On the mountain above the cave
Had one been seen, heard or known
This would not be Claude the Noble's grave.

Claude the Noble led his army
Five thousand men all loyal and brave.
The rocks crashed down in a mighty fury
When they'd been not long in the cave.

Three weeks hence they moved the stones.
A great foul stench filled the air.
Not a soul lived, not one found
To escape fortune's cruel lair

"Thus the riches of Earth will you reap."
Was not my fate nor did I fail.
For I have stood with Claude the Noble
And I alone have returned to tell the tale.

Aunt Sam: 2014

by Gene Curtis

The large screen covering the wall in front of console 3 showed the aerial view of the city from strato-platform 3 stationed 10 miles overhead. A bright red dot flashed in the upper left corner. Rosetta thought the activity was pretty slow for a Monday morning, this was just the sixth alarm so far. She punched a few keys and brought up the interior view of the bank. The black and white image showed three people wearing ski masks and waving handguns. She reached over, pushed a large red button and spoke into her headset, "Scramble, scramble, scramble. Team 3, your vector is…" Her fingers tapped more keys and the overhead view came back up on the screen and was overlaid with a polar grid showing one radial highlighted and the number 217 flashing at the bottom center. "Two-one-seven at three miles. Team 3, scramble, scramble, scramble. Your vector is two-one-seven at three miles. Armed bank robbery in progress, three suspects with handguns, wearing dark ski masks and dark jump suits."

She tapped a few more keys, and an image of the ready room appeared inset on the screen. The room could have been mistaken for a standard break room in any medium to large office complex, except for the six tables sporting computer consoles with three wired visors each. Team 1 was seated around their console and was just finishing up from a high speed chase and returning to base. Team 2 was in the middle of a hostage situation. A peeping tom had been able to elude capture in a foot chase after being spotted using a ladder to peep into a second story bathroom to watch a young teen get ready for school. His path took him past a bus stop where he grabbed a kid and was now holding a knife to the kid's throat. Bill, lead member of Team 2, had landed his helicopter on a nearby roof, giving him a good view of the situation and allowing him to conserve fuel. The helicopters had enough fuel for an hour of flight, a few minutes more if the cameras and equipment were jettisoned early enough.

Team 3 walked to their station, donned helmets and took their seats. The split screen on their console showed the heads-up display from each of the helmets and the tactical map for their specific mission. Team 3's leader, Jen, said, "John, you take intercept 1. Jean you're on intercept 2, and I'll fly primary."

Each of the 6 teams consisted of 3 members. Intercept 1 was the designation for the member whose mission was to get on the scene post-haste, identify and mark the bad guys for initial tracking and, if needed, run interference until the proper authorities could step in. Intercept 1's platform of choice was usually a high speed, variable wing aircraft. Intercept 2 was the designation for the member whose mission was to tag the bad guys with some form of tracking device that would give the bad guy's specific location in most situations. This was usually done by deploying a GPS tracker, and the usual platform of choice was a fixed wing, high speed aircraft. Primary was the designation for the team leader whose mission was to monitor circumstances in situations where other platforms had diminished ability. The platform of choice was usually a rotorcraft with a payload of multiple electronic devices that could be deployed in unusual circumstances.

John said, "I'm seeing 36 seconds to intercept from launch. Con, I'm go on you're order."

Jean said, "Intercept 2, I make it 2 minutes thirty seconds to target. Launch on your order Con."

Jen said, "Six minutes for primary on target Con."

Rosetta responded, "Con copy. Intercept 1, stand by. Primary, launch, launch, launch."

Jen replied, "Primary launched, vectoring two-one-seven, 100 AGL, low and slow."

Rosetta switched to the inside view at the bank and waited for the robbers to start making their exit. "Intercept 1, launch, launch, launch. Three suspects confirmed, heading out the front door."

"Intercept 1 away, two one seven at 500 AGL. Get me a target."

Rosetta switched to the overhead view and zoomed in the image. "They're getting into a gray SUV, an older model, and pulling out north on Wiltshire. Intercept 2, launch, launch, launch."

"Intercept 2, I'm airborne."

"Intercept 1, coming up on target area... I've got it, vectoring for a shot... cameras rolling... license plate is Alpha-Mike-Kilo, Juliet-Charlie-Kilo... making a paint pass... target is painted."

"Intercept 1, I see your paint, come on home."

"Vectoring one-zero-five at 500 AGL, heading for base."

Rosetta said, "Intercept 2, climb to 2000, get a fix and launch a tracker."

A few seconds later, Jean said, "Intercept 2 at 2000, target locked and tracker is away." A moment later she said, "Tracker is attached and working."

John said, "Intercept 1 is back and docked."

Rosetta looked at the bottom of the screen and saw the GPS coordinates of the getaway vehicle. "Intercept 2, Con confirms, we have tracking. Intercept 2, come on home. Primary climb to 3000 and monitor."

"Roger Con, Intercept 2 vectoring one-two-zero for home."

"Primary copy, climbing to 3000."

Sam walked up and looked at the screen. "Another tag well done." She opened her cell phone and dialed 911.

"Hi. I think there was a robbery at the bank on Wiltshire, and I'm following the getaway car... Yes, the plate number is AMK-JCK... It's a gray SUV, a Dodge I think, an older one... It's heading out of town on Wiltshire... No, it's not speeding or anything... Yes ma'am, I know it's dangerous; I just want you to catch them... I can't really see, but I think there's three of them... yes ma'am, I will." Sam closed the phone, smiled at Rosetta and went back to her desk.

A few key taps brought a view of Adrian to her screen. He was seated at a console in the back of a van and looking rather bored. His cameras were trained on the area where a new street dealer was working. He had determined the dealer had three stashes, one at the base of a large oak tree, another under a drain pipe on the corner of the nearby apartment building and the third in the tall grass around the base of a nearby fire hydrant.

Sam said, "How're you doing?"

"I haven't seen it this slow in a long time; just 10 since sunup."

"We need a hundred or it won't stand up."

The local judges had taken a severe dislike to the concept of private citizens routinely spying on and video taping anyone, even drug dealers, with the intent of using that footage in a court of law. Nothing this group was doing was technically illegal, but the judges, as a group, set the rule that there had to be at least a hundred confirmed incidents to establish intent beyond a reasonable doubt. The confirmed part was easy enough to prove, all it took was identifying what was being sold. Waiting for the buyers to show up was usually pretty quick. Once Adrian had taped more than a hundred buys, he would call the police and give the dispatcher the details of how the dealer was working and where his stash was. When the officers showed up, the video would find its way onto a driver's seat in one of their cars.

"I know. It looks like it's going to be a long day."

"Same here. I'll check on you again later. Command Center out."

Sam switched to the word processing program, printed out her letter of resignation, looked it over, signed it, put it in an envelope, and then put it in the top drawer of her desk. She got up and went to console 2; the hostage situation was still going on.

"Tell Bill he's authorized to use a hornet." She knew full well she had just ordered a set of events that would almost certainly lead to the bad guy's death. It wasn't a decision she made lightly.

The hornet was just what its name implied, a small winged platform that was difficult to distinguish from a real Japanese hornet, unless you could get a good close look at it. The standard procedure was to launch it out-of-sight, but as close as possible to the target. Its power cell provided about five minutes of flight time. A team member would pilot it in close to the suspect and distract him long enough for the police to do their job. If buzzing the target didn't work then landing on him and/or stinging him usually did the trick. The sting was nothing more than a very small chemical burn caused by a miniscule drop of acid, crude but effective. In this case it was likely the police would take their shots as soon as the guy moved the knife away from the kid's throat. They did.

She'd seen this scenario played out too many times over the years. Still, it wasn't her choice to hold a knife to that little boy's throat, but it was her choice to do what she could to see to it he survived. It was her choice to do what she could to keep the bad guys from winning. Anyway, that was what this whole operation was about, keeping the bad guys from winning. It just didn't sit well with her the way things were going, and overall, they were going too fast.

She walked over to console 4. "Has Court left yet?"

Court Tremens was her companion. Twelve years had passed since Shawn, her husband, had been shot down. *My God, has it really been twelve years?* Court and Shawn had been best friends since grade school, and he took the news almost as hard as she did. In the few months that followed, Court had been just the right someone to hold when she needed to hold someone. Their relationship grew from there, and now he was her second husband in every way that counted, just not on paper. *No, not on paper, that will never happen.*

Juanita tapped a few keys and worked her joystick. The aerial view zoomed to a single residence on the outskirts of town and showed a red '67 Mustang convertible in the driveway. It had a big smiley face painted on the trunk with infrared paint, invisible to the naked eye, but very visible to the eyes overhead.

The strato-platforms, eight in all, and each with six cameras, were almost impossible to see from the ground and were designed that way to make them hard targets to hit with small arms fire, a necessity discovered in the early years. Being out-of-sight was also effectively out-of-mind. The platforms held station at 10 miles high now, well out of range of small arms, and no longer needed the stealth design, but Sam had decided it was a good idea to keep the old design.

Juanita said, "No, ma'am, it's still a few minutes too early. Do you want me to let you know when he leaves?"

Sam's cell phone rang. She nodded at Juanita while she answered the phone. "Hello."

"Ms. Goodman, this is David Mead at the front gate. There's a delivery truck here with six boxes and a large envelope for you. I'm not showing any expected deliveries for today."

"We're not expecting any packages. Who're they from?"

"The routing slip just has a number code, and there's no marking on the boxes."

Sam's computer beeped twice, indicating she had just received an e-mail. She started walking to her desk. "Let me speak to the delivery person." She brought up the new message while she waited.

Hi Sam,

Just a little taste of some of the things you'll be getting when you say yes. You just received six machines that will let you compress a week's worth of video to one disk and some image enhancement software, all next generation stuff. You get to keep it either way.

Badger

Col. Barnes, I should've known. Col. Barnes made it perfectly clear why he was courting her operation; intelligence information on people in the United States was a rare and valuable commodity in the spy world, especially so for Homeland Security. He went to great pains to search her out and let her know he would be happy to accept information that she might want to *volunteer* for the good of the country. He couldn't ask for it directly, and paying for it was out of the question, but defense contractors, a lot of defense contractors, were always looking for places to field test their *next generation* products. They were also encouraged to make tax deductible contributions to, shall we say, select non-profit organizations.

Her answer was not the one he wanted to accept, and she could give none other in good conscience. Looking for criminal actions in public places was one thing, but collecting information on targeted individuals who hadn't committed a crime as yet was an entirely different one, a highly illegal one. Sure this operation bordered on the fringes of the illegal line sometimes, especially the practice of tagging targets with GPS trackers, but if it ever came up, the public good outweighed the criminal's expectation of privacy; at least that's what the corporation's lawyers said.

A different voice came over the phone, "Hello."

"Hi. Can you tell me where these packages came from?"

"I just drive the truck, ma'am. I load the boxes at the warehouse and take them to the address on the label."

"I see. Thank you."

David came back over the phone. "What do you want me to do with them?"

"Have someone bring them here."

"Yes, ma'am."

Sam looked back at the computer screen, the message from Col. Barnes was gone. She checked the list of recent emails, and it wasn't there either. She shook her head. *This game of secret squirrel isn't amusing, Colonel.*

Juanita called across the room, "He's leaving now. Do you want me to give him the traffic report?"

Sam looked up. "I'll call him. Is there anything working right now."

"Just an accident on the interstate; traffic's down to one lane."

Sam finished her call and went to console 3. Rosetta said, "Jen's still up; the robbery suspects are taking what looks like a random course through the back roads, no way they can lay down a puncture strip. There're six patrol cars giving chase: three locals, two sheriffs and one state trooper."

Sam looked at the map overlay. "I'll bet they're heading back to town to try and lose them in traffic. Tell Jen to stay with it." She dialed the police dispatcher.

"Hi, this is Samantha Goodman at Cousin Inc. We're watching the chase, and it looks like they're heading back to town. We think they're going to try to tie up traffic to effect their getaway. There's only two places where they might have a chance at succeeding; East Andover at Hermitage, or Harrison's Corner. The only other thing that might work is if they go off-road." She looked at the map overlay on the screen again. "Hold on just a second." She held the phone down and pointed to the map and said to Juanita, "Take a close look here for off-road paths."

The view on the screen pulled back, swept ahead of the chase and zoomed back in to an area known locally as the mudflats. It was a maze of muddy paths intertwined amid the trees and hills on the south shore of Lake Prince. Rosetta said, "If they get in there, you'd need a four wheel drive to follow them."

"Pull back, and let's see where they might be planning to come out." The view pulled back, and Sam spotted a small boat on the shore next to the mudflats. She pointed and said, "There, let me have a closer look at that."

There was a guy sitting in a small speed boat, talking on a cell phone. "Give me a wide view of the whole area." The screen pulled back, and Sam traced the robbers' original path on Wiltshire to its closest approach to the lake and saw the dead end road leading to a small boat launch ramp on the northwest shore of the lake. She pointed and said, "Let me see here." There was a single white truck with a boat trailer in the parking lot.

Sam brought the phone back up. "Is there a game warden working Lake Prince today?"

The dispatcher said, "We don't have anyone out there right now. What are you seeing?"

"There's a boat waiting on the south shore of Lake Prince right next to the mudflats, and I'll bet that's where they're heading. They have a four wheel drive vehicle, and it makes perfect sense. And there's just one truck at the boat ramp on the northwest shore, just off Wiltshire."

"Got it. I'll get some units to that boat ramp and see if the state has a game warden on the lake today."

Sam closed the phone. "Tell Jen to get some altitude if they turn into the woods, and if they stop, make a note of the coordinates."

Sam and Rosetta watched the bad guys make three more turns and head straight for the mudflats. Sam said, "Get a number 2 intercept up and tag that truck at the boat ramp."

Rosetta tapped a few keys and spoke into her headset, "Team 3, intercept 2, scramble, scramble, scramble. Your vector is three four zero at twelve miles. Your target is a white truck with a boat trailer, the only one in the parking lot. Tag and return, launch when ready."

Jean responded, "Intercept 2 is airborne, ten minutes to target."

Sam said, "Authorize her for hot burn. We don't have ten minutes before the patrol cars get there."

Rosetta said, "Intercept 2, you are authorized for hot burn. Kick it, girl, we don't have ten minutes."

Jean said, "Roger Con, time to target is five. Woo-who!"

Rosetta kept a wide view of the mudflats and the boat. The police cars giving chase turned around, fast heading back toward Wiltshire and were quickly off the screen. The getaway vehicle couldn't be seen through the canopy, but the GPS readout showed constant movement, and a red dot indicated its position on the overlay. A few minutes passed before three figures could be seen scrambling for the boat.

Jen said, "I'm orbiting at 3000, and I'm not seeing any traffic on the water."

Rosetta said, "Con copy." She pulled back on the joystick, widening the view. "Primary, I'm showing a single craft on the water inbound at six miles on zero four five your position. I make its speed at about 30 knots, ETA 12 minutes." She zoomed in on the craft. "It's the state game warden."

Sam dialed the police dispatcher again. "Hi, this is Sam Goodman again. Can you contact the game warden on the lake and have him change course for the boat ramp on the northeast shore? He'll be looking for a green over white tri-hull, I'd say about a fifteen footer, heading that way. If he tries to catch it on the shore by the mudflats, he'll miss it by about ten minutes."

The dispatcher said, "I'll relay the message."

Sam said, "They've just now shoved off. If they start heading anywhere but that boat ramp, I'll call you back."

"Thanks, I've got two units that should be getting to the ramp any moment now. If the boat changes course, let me know ASAP."

"We'll do it."

Sam asked Rosetta, "How close is Jane to target?"

"Intercept 2, what's your status?"

"Con, I have a visual... tracker is away... target is tagged, standing down from hot burn and returning to base. Con, I'm seeing two jellybeans inbound." A few years back, when the new style, rounded police cars first appeared on the streets, someone commented that they looked like high-speed attack jellybeans. The nickname stuck.

"Con copy, climb out fast before you're spotted."

"Copy Con, climbing to 3000."

Rosetta turned the camera back to the getaway boat. It was on a bearing straight for the boat ramp and making about 40 knots. A half mile from the ramp the boat came to a complete stop.

Rosetta said, "They've spotted the police." She zoomed in, and the four guys were obviously having a heated discussion. The boat swung around and started back toward the mud flats. It didn't get very far before it swung back around and started a course due north. Rosetta pulled back and saw the game warden coming in.

Sam dialed the dispatcher. "The boat is heading due north from the boat ramp. It looks like they're headed for Sterling Point."

"That's what the officers at the ramp just radioed in. Can you get a look at 1439 Seymour Drive? That's where the white truck is registered."

Sam put her hand over the phone. "Bring up 1439 Seymour Drive."

The screen switched to a different view and swept in. Sam spoke into the phone. "It's a vacant lot."

"Thanks, that saves me from having to send a unit. Can you stay on the phone and keep me updated on the boat?"

"I'll do better than that; bring up our website, and we'll stream the video. It'll be on camera 3, the password is Aunt Sam." Sam leaned toward console 4 and whispered to Juanita, "Patch your console's main view into web cam 3 and follow the boat, but don't get in too close; I don't want to let them know how much we can do."

Juanita nodded.

Sam said to the dispatcher, "The feed should be live any moment now. We'll follow them as long as we can."

The boat passed Sterling Point, went up Paradise Creek a short distance and started heading for the east shore. The area was a wetland, thick with trees and undergrowth. Visual tracking would be impossible.

Sam said, "Tell Jen to deploy ticks."

Ticks were tiny electronic chips designed to stick to fabric and give a return signal when illuminated with terahertz energy, radio wave above the normal microwave frequencies and lower than infrared frequencies.

Rosetta said, "Get some ticks on them before they get into the woods."

Jen said, "Setting dispersal pattern alpha at 200 feet. Capsule is away… missed. Setting capsule 2 for pattern alpha at 100 feet. Number two is away… on target, subjects are tagged."

Rosetta tapped a few keys and said, "T-wave illumination is active." She looked at the screen and saw the crowd of blips, several of which were moving. "We have tracking. I'm patching the feed to your display."

"Copy con, climbing back to 3000."

Juanita pulled back for a wide view. "Where do you think they're heading?"

Sam said, "I don't think it matters. If they can get K-9 in there fast enough, they can drive them out wherever they want." Sam pointed out the three K-9 vehicles approaching on the other side of the woods. "Zoom back in, not too close and see if you can get a glimpse of them."

Rosetta said, "They've stopped." She zoomed in and couldn't see anything but trees. "I'm going to try thermal." The image switched and showed shapes in varying colors. "They're not just stopped, they're doing something." She noted their coordinates.

Sam said, "Juanita, locate the closest blimp, fly it in and get right over them. And switch off your feed to web cam 3."

Cousin Inc. had 48 blimps flying over the city at any given time, all on preprogrammed courses between 500 and 1000 feet above ground level, each carrying cameras and a huge LED screen, essentially a high definition television screen on which advertising space was sold. They also served as aerial platforms for proprietary news feeds when needed. Most people thought that they were the source for the surveillance footage often used by the police as an aid to investigations. Few knew the true source of the footage was from the strato-platforms. No one outside the hand picked operators and top echelon personnel at Cousin Inc. knew of the remote control flight operations either, and that's the way they wanted to keep it.

Sam dialed the police dispatcher. "Hi, this is Sam Goodman. We're flying one of our blimps down into the area where they are. It'll give your units a visual reference."

The dispatcher said, "Thanks, I'll tell them."

Sam closed the phone and looked at the screen. She remembered the first time she had flown a remote controlled aircraft with a video camera in the cockpit. The plane was so heavy it almost didn't get off the ground. Thirty plus years had seen quite a change in technology. The same capabilities today were about the size and weight of a small key chain light now, nothing more than a mere toy. She had grown this operation from that humble beginning and, at this point, was prepared to just walk out if the board of directors voted against her wishes. *That pompous, pontificating, paper-pushing Col. Barnes thinks he can convince me that it's right to use this company to get the goods on potential terrorists. Potential terrorist—you might as well be saying suspected communists back in the fifties. It's the same thing. Spy on people who haven't done anything, create fear and suspicion based on innuendo and supposition. That's about as unpatriotic as it gets. Didn't he swear to defend the Constitution? Doesn't he understand that if any covert operation the company does goes wrong, more than ten thousand families stand to lose their homes and livelihoods? And for what, just to make his job a little easier? I'll have no part of it.*

Juanita said, "What are those light flashes?"

Rosetta answered, "Gunfire."

Sam asked, "Who's doing the shooting?"

"The suspects. The K-9 officers must be closing in. The bad guys are splitting up."

Sam said, "Juanita, switch to thermal."

Screen 4 changed to showing striations of color. Picking out variations that might be people was difficult through the sun heated canopy. A person had to remain in the same relative area for a minute or two to create a signature distinctive enough to be recognized.

Juanita said, "I can't make out anything."

Sam said, "That's because everyone is still moving." Two purple spots started forming at the top of the screen. She pointed and said, "Give me a ping right there."

A moment later ever decreasing concentric circles flashed on and off highlighting the area.

"Rosetta, have Jen get a hornet in there."

Rosetta said, "Primary, launch a hornet, your target is the ping."

Jen said, "Autopilot on, launching hornet. What am I looking for?"

Sam leaned in and pushed a button on the console. "Jen, I think there might be an officer down. I need confirmation."

"Roger Con, I'm in now. Con, that is confirmed, officer down. He's bleeding on his right arm, shoulder and head. His dog is down too. I'm sending in a rescue beacon, channel A."

Sam said, "Con copy." She dialed the dispatcher. "I think you might have an officer down. We saw flashes that could have been gunfire, and now we're showing a thermal image not moving."

The dispatcher said, "Our officers are reporting shots fired, but they can't get a fix on the location."

"Tell the medics to track rescue beacon channel A, and if your officers can see the blimp go toward it. We'll drop it down lower so they can hear it."

"Good deal, I'll tell them."

Sam hung up. "Juanita, push your engines to full and get in as low as you can right over the ping."

Rosetta said, "I'm only tracking three suspects, two could be together, but I don't think so. One's heading back toward the boat, and two are separated, heading generally northeast. Ah, there he is. Number 4 is stationary where they split up."

Sam's phone rang. "Hello."

"Hi. This is Don Wilkerson at Channel 7 News. Can we get a feed on the police chase off Lake Prince?"

"Sure, standard rates. The feed will be coming through on line 6."

"Got it. Thanks."

"Tony, swing blimp 8 around to cover the chase for Channel 7 News. Patch the feed through your primary line."

A news feed was how Cousin Inc. had started. Sam had driven her van to a three alarm fire and launched her new blimp to watch the action from above. An on-scene reporter saw what she was doing and kept upping the offer for a live feed. Sam finally said yes when the bid was ridiculously high. News feeds became a minor revenue stream for the company. The primary stream came from the small monthly fee she charged the 10,000 plus area businesses for 24/7 surveillance. It wasn't a hard sell—the business's insurance premiums dropped more than enough to cover the cost, and over a short time burglaries were down more than ninety percent. Almost overnight she was making millions.

Sam hung up and dialed the dispatcher. "Hi, this is Sam Goodman again. We think the suspects have split up; two are heading generally northeast, and one might be trying to make it back to the boat. It might be a good idea to give the game warden a heads-up. We're not sure where the fourth suspect is. There's a thermal image near where your officers are heading, but we can't tell if it's him or not."

"Thanks, I'll relay the information. Any chance of getting you to stay on the line?"

"As much as I've been calling, it might be a good idea. The image you were getting was from the blimp I sent down," Sam lied. "As soon as you get some officers on scene, I'll send it back up."

"You can go ahead and send it back up, an officer is arriving now."

Sam lowered the phone and said, "Juanita, take the blimp back up and switch the feed back on to the web cam. Stay with the chase. Same rules as before."

Rosetta said, "The game warden is towing the boat out."

Sam asked, "Which targets are you tracking?"

"All three, I'm switching back and forth."

"Tony, light up the suspect heading for the boat and route that camera into console 3. Juanita, you light up the northern most guy and tie that feed to console 3. Both of you exclude your primary feeds."

Juanita said, "I haven't done anything like this before—any suggestions?"

Tony said, "Go to a split-screen mode and tie the T-ray tracking to your secondary camera. Look at Rosetta's screen to adjust your aim point."

"Got it. Thanks."

Rosetta said, "The one heading for the boat has stopped just short of the shore. The game warden sees him and is pointing a shotgun at him. The guy's looking back into the woods."

Sam put the phone to her ear. "The one—"

The dispatcher said, "I heard. A K-9 officer is closing in. He should be in custody in a few minutes."

"How much can you hear?"

"Don't worry, I don't understand most of the technical stuff, and besides, it wouldn't do me a bit of good to make you mad. I'm not saying anything to anybody. I do have a lot more confidence in what you're telling me now. You might be interested in knowing that the other suspect is DRT."

"DRT?"

"Sorry, it's police slang, dead right there."

"I see. How's the officer and his dog?"

"He's going to live. One bullet went up his arm, out his shoulder and grazed his head, nothing vital. The dog took three to the head and chest."

Rosetta said, "The one by the boat is making a run for it. The game warden just fired twice. He's still running, but he threw his gun down. There's the K-9 officer. He's let the dog loose. The dog's after him. Got him! Ooo, I bet that hurts."

Tony said, "Channel 7 is going to love that."

Sam said, "There's still two more."

Rosetta said, "Pulling back. The southern one is moving toward Sterling Point, and the northern one has turned due north. It looks like he might come out behind Triangle Shopping Center."

Sam said, "ETA's?"

"Assuming they maintain the same direction and pace, I'd say the southern guy will exit around the 200 block of Wycliff Drive in about 7 minutes, and the northern guy is about 13 minutes from the shopping center."

Sam put the phone back to her ear. "Did you get that?"

"I've got three units near Wycliff now and more are in route."

"Are there any units moving toward the shopping center?"

"Every available unit is moving into the area."

Rosetta said, "I'm seeing a SWAT van pulling into the shopping center now, and Bill is flying a replacement out to Jean; she'll be off line for a few seconds while they switch."

The dispatcher said to Sam, "The SWAT team is just standing by in case they're needed."

Rosetta said, "The guy near Wycliff has stopped near the edge of the woods—

wait, he's doubling back. Now he's stopped about thirty yards in."

Sam said, "Can Jean get a hornet in there yet?"

Jean said, "I'm five minutes out."

The dispatcher said, "My K-9 officer says he's climbed up into a tree house. He's not going anywhere."

Sam said, "The southern guy is treed; let's get on the northern guy."

Rosetta said, "He's turned back to the northeast, heading for the high school."

Sam thought, *This guy is probably thinking he can cut through the school to slow up the K-9 officer and then make it to the road and hijack a car. He's in for a surprise when he sees all the cops heading his way. What are his choices? He can't double back. If he gets trapped in the school, that's no good. He could turn and keep running for it, but it would be just a matter of moments before he was caught. He could stand and fight, but that's a losing option. Crap, his best choice is the school.*

Sam said to the dispatcher, "Call the school and give them a heads up. I'll call you back."

She hung up and dialed Court's phone. There was no answer. She remembered he had to keep it turned off during classes. He was the science and math teacher for the gifted and talented students. Every day a couple of the other area high schools would ship their best students here for the advanced math and science classes. Court applied for the job when he retired from the air force and was surprised when he got it.

An Interlude

by Barbara Hatcher Shaver

Josephine's short red hair is standing on edge this morning from yesterday's leftover anger. She grabs item after item and keys each price into her cash register. *That new checker is starting off at $4.00 an hour, and he's only a high school student.* Peering at her customer through silver-rimmed glasses, Josephine spits through her gum, "That'll be forty dollars and thirteen cents."

Josephine leans over the counter and catches a glimpse of one of her turquoise and silver dangling earrings while her customer fumbles with his money. *Where is that bagger? I'm not putting these groceries in bags. Look at that line. Will he ever get his money out of his pocket?* Josephine's lips become round as she purses them tighter, and her peaked nose reddens as she becomes more agitated.

"How much did you say my bill is?" the old man says, looking up at her.

Josephine raises her voice and says, "Forty dollars and thirteen cents."

"Here's a twenty and two tens. No, one of them is only a five," he says slowly and then opens his hand, revealing two dollars and the change, a dime and three pennies. Reaching in his pants pockets, he pulls the lining out of one side and then the other, looking for more money.

"I'll have to put something back," he says. "That's all the money I have."

Josephine looks at his order. Yesterday's reduced meat, a small bag of potatoes, a few oranges and apples, some lunch meat and tomatoes, about a dozen assorted cans, a carton of milk, and a loaf of bread.

She looks at him, too. His face is scruffy and unshaven. He is thin and frail. His coat is hanging off his shoulders; his belt is buckled in a homemade hole. *He probably just moved into those cheap apartments down the road.* Josephine turns her head towards the office. The manager is peering at them through the open door.

"You gonna give this man three dollars, aren't you?"

"Why, yes, of course," the manager replies while glaring at her.

Josephine takes the old gentleman's money and puts it in the register. She turns around and bags his groceries after all.

While she is checking the next customer's groceries, Josephine thinks about the old man. *I don't remember seeing him in here before. Well, everything is changing. A movie theater used to be on this spot.* She smiles to herself as she remembers sitting in the theater on Saturday afternoons as a child and holding hands in it on Saturday nights as a teenager. Customers go through her line, one by one. Josephine routinely does her job, smiling and thanking each one. When things go smoothly, the job's thinkless for Josephine. Today's reminiscing is not so unlike that of many other days she has spent on the job. For some thirty years, ever since she was sixteen, she has worked for Scotford Grocery in southern Georgia, a short distance from Atlanta. Many of the store's customers know Josephine, and she is a likeable person.

Getting lost in her thoughts again, Josephine gazes outside. Across the street she sees a new store that just opened. Cars are coming and going on the newly-paved highway. She notices dark clouds gathering slowly above the parking lot. A short while later, the store lights flicker as lightning flashes, followed by a roll of thunder.

"We're getting a storm, another one of those late summer ones," Josephine says to her customer as the flickering lights bounce her thoughts back to reality. "I hate storms. I'm scared to death of 'em."

"Well, you're safe in here," her customer offers.

Josephine's hands continue grasping groceries, something like a hawk swooping down and flying away with its prey. She reads the price on each item and keys it into her cash register.

"Oh, I know I'm pretty safe if I'm inside during a storm," she says rolling her eyes to the upper left. "But then there was this time I was sitting on the sofa in our living room as a child and saw a ball of fire shoot straight through the middle of the room during a storm. Mama had said, 'Sit down and be quiet, Josephine Sue. This is God's work.'"

"I don't like the wind," her customer says while tapping her pen on her checkbook.

"I'm not talking about the wind, honey." Josephine chomps hard on her gum. "I guess everybody feels scared and defenseless during a wind storm, 'specially a tornado or a hurricane. There's not much any of us can do to protect ourselves if the wind gets fierce enough, but to pray, maybe," Josephine's voice cracks. "No, I'm talking about a regular old thunderstorm. I don't know if my fear started when that ball of fire shot through our living room or when I got caught out in a storm once as a child." Josephine gives her customer some change and says hello to the next person in line. She continues talking, not giving her new customer a chance to say anything.

"I loved walking on our farm when I was a child. Almost every time I went outside, I'd soon find myself on the dirt path that led through the woods behind our house. I'd skip over the roots of this old oak tree, the one my grandfather said had stood there for a century or more. Under the shade of that tree, the roots looked just like stair steps. It felt comfortable and right to follow them to the field beyond. The day I was caught in the thunderstorm, I was skipping on the roots when I stumbled. Afraid that I would fall, I grabbed onto a small tree and sat down hard at the base of its trunk. While sitting there alone, I realized it was beginning to get dark. I remember thinking a storm's coming and I was too far from home to risk going back."

Josephine continues talking as she checks groceries. She is oblivious to the fact that her customer is getting agitated with her. "Josephine, you have customers," snapped the manager as he marches from his office. He is at his best when annoying someone, and he is good at intimidating Josephine. "I want to see you in my office when you get off."

Josephine stiffens as her eyes catch his, then she turns immediately to her customer.

"Oh, I'm sorry. 'Scuse me, Ma'am."

"Oh, that's all right. We all have certain things that get us upset," her customer offers.

Josephine works her last fifteen minutes, and then makes her way into the manager's office. The wind continues picking up outside.

"What do you mean asking me to give that old man three dollars, and what's the big idea of standing there talking instead of giving your customers your full attention? I'm running a business, not a remember-when tea party."

"Don't talk to me about three dollars with all the money you make," Josephine leans over his desk. Her voice hits his ears like a kettledrum.

"Three dollars here; two dollars there. You're always asking me to give money away. That's unfair, and it eats into the store's profits."

"Oh, for goodness sakes, what's three dollars to you? You own this whole store," Josephine says as she points her finger. "What profit do I get? I'll tell you what's unfair: I've worked here for thirty years, since 1952, and I get paid only $6.50 an hour. Now, that's unfair. The high school student I trained yesterday started out at $4.00 an hour? How you gonna explain that?"

"Uh, I can't get anybody to work for cheaper than that."

"Oh, yeah, and you can get me to work for cheap," Josephine booms. "What has thirty years gotten me? Nothing. I don't even enjoy eating. Working around food all the time takes my appetite." With that said, Josephine leaves his office and walks outside into the impending storm.

Josephine's burdens feel heavy as she makes her way to her car. She opens the door with a strong jerk and gets inside. Her 1973 Oldsmobile station wagon offers her its familiar security as she sits down. The driver's seat fits snugly to her back; she leans against it and stretches out her legs. Feeling exhausted, Josephine's body needs to relax. But she can't just yet. *If that manager hadn't called me into his office, I would be home by now and out of this storm.*

With rain pelting her windshield and the wipers whacking big drops back and forth, Josephine slowly pulls out onto the highway. With her defrost on high, she peers through the windshield and drives slowly through the green traffic light. About two miles down the road, Josephine spots someone walking and carrying bags. As she gets closer, Josephine sees through the curtain of rain on her windshield that it is her customer, the old man. With his shoulders bent, he is trudging through puddles and getting drenched.

Josephine pulls over, rolls down her window, and asks him if he wants a ride. He hesitates, but then catches a glimpse of her face. Remembering her from the grocery store, he says, "Oh, thank you, Ma'am."

"Where do you live?"

"You turn right at the next light, and then I live just up that road and around a curve. Do you live out that way?"

"No, you go straight at the light to get to my house."

"Well, just put me out at the corner, then. I can walk the rest of the way."

"Nonsense, I'll take you home." *He lives just where I thought.* Josephine drives on in silence. She slowly pulls into the driveway of the apartment complex.

"Thank you a lot. Won't you come in?"

"No, I'd better get on home, out of this storm. See you around the store…"

"I'd really like to fix you a cup of coffee, or something. Can't you come in?"

"Well, since you put it like that, maybe I will. A cup of coffee would taste good and would warm my bones. By the way, I'm Josephine. What's your name?" Josephine asks as they walk towards the apartment door.

"Emmett's my name. Have a seat while I get the coffee going and get these groceries put away."

I'll just sit here in this straight back chair and leave the sofa for him. Wonder where his bedroom is? I don't see any doors except for the bathroom there off the kitchen. I bet he has to sleep on the sofa. What's that standing over there in the corner? Fishing poles, maybe?

"Aren't those fishing poles over there, Emmett? You ever do any fishing?"

"Yeah, they're my reed poles. I've had them since I was a boy. Once when my grandfather came to see us, he brought them to me and told me he'd made them from these tall reeds that grew alongside his shed. I've kept them all these years, had to put new line on them a coupla times, that's all. Yeah, I fish a little. Would you like to go sometime?" Emmett says as he pours Josephine a cup of coffee and offers her the milk and sugar.

"I'll have a little milk, just enough to change the color," Josephine says. She wraps her hands around the cup, enjoying its warmth as she takes a sip. "Thank you, Emmett, the coffee tastes good."

"Do you think you'd like to go fishing?"

"Well, maybe. I haven't been since I was a child. We, my brother and I, that is, used to fish in the fishpond on our farm. Sometime daddy fished with us, but he was usually busy working several different farm jobs. I don't own a rod and reel."

"Well, you can use one of my poles. I'll also furnish the bait. When would you like to go?"

"I'm off on Thursday, day after tomorrow. How's that for you?"

"That's fine with me. I'll check out my lines and floaters tomorrow, make sure everything is in good shape."

"You like to go early?"

"Yeah, I like to get there before the sun gets too hot."

"How about if I pick you up about 7:00?"

"Okay, but do you know where we can go?"

"There's a river on down this road a piece. I hear people in the store talk about going there. Maybe we'll try it," Josephine says as she gets up to leave.

"Sounds good to me."

"Thanks for the coffee."

Josephine waves as she drives off.

Josephine gets up early on Thursday morning and steps outside to check the weather. The air is a little nippy. She dresses in old jeans and a tee shirt with a plaid shirt buttoned over it. She ties a kerchief around her head and puts on her usual red lipstick. In a way that she can't explain, Josephine is looking forward to this fishing trip. She's never really liked fishing. It was just something they did for fun in the summer when she was growing up. For winter fun, they sat rabbit boxes in the snow.

Her father would say, "Here, Josephine. I made you and John new rabbit boxes yesterday. Let's take them and set them out after breakfast." Josephine's father always said to cut an apple in half and rub some of its juices at the trap door of the wooden rectangle box. Then, he'd tell them to throw a piece inside the box so when a rabbit smelled the scent and went in to get the apple, he'd hit the lever causing the door to fall, trapping himself. As far as Josephine could remember, they had never caught a rabbit, but it had been fun trying. In fact, she didn't think she'd ever caught a fish either, but she guessed she'd give it a try this morning.

On the way to Emmett's, Josephine turns off the road and into the parking lot of the country store where she likes to stop and buy a cup of coffee whenever she is out this way. *The parking lot wasn't paved when I was here before. I had to drive through mud puddles once when it had rained.* Inside, the store is different, too; chrome cabinets replace wooden shelves, neon lights overshadow fluorescent bulbs, and the benches are gone. *There's no place to sit to enjoy my coffee.*

"Whacha need?" the stocky person behind the counter says.

"I'll have a cup of coffee, please."

"That'll be fifty cents. There it is over there. Fix your own."

"Well, whatever happened to the thirty-five cents cup of coffee and the nice person with the friendly smile?"

"Whacha mean?"

"The other man, Lewis, smiled as he poured my coffee for me. Many people would be in here, too, sitting around on benches. What did you do with the wooden benches, sell them?"

"Well, everything changes, ya know."

"Yeah, well, some things do."

With her coffee in hand, Josephine makes her way back across the pavement, which is beginning to dry after an early morning shower. She notices the telephone pole that once held a security light is gone, having been replaced by two chrome poles with long narrow lights. Josephine hears the sizzling tires of the highway traffic as she gets into her car.

Driving in silence, Josephine tries making sense of some things. *Has another child discovered the roots and skips over them? What happened to thirty years of my life? What am I going to do about my boss or my job? Why did Emmett move here?*

Always punctual, it is 7:00 a.m. when Josephine pulls into the driveway at Emmett's apartment. She notices a light in his ground-floor room. Taking her coffee with her, Josephine walks up to the door and knocks. She peers through the glass and sees Emmett coming towards her. *He looks different after a good night's sleep.* "Come in, gal. I'm making our dough balls now."

"You're making what?"

"Dough balls. That's what I fish with, the best bait you can find. You just mix flour, water, and salt with a little lard and knead it into dough. Then you pinch off pieces and roll them into balls like I'm doing. I always put them in an old bread wrapper like this, keeps them from drying out. You want to help?"

Josephine and Emmett finish making the dough balls together. The long fishing poles Josephine had seen the day before are leaning against the kitchen table, ready for their day of fishing. "You reckon we'll catch anything?" Josephine asks as she wipes dough off her fingers.

"I think so. I feel awfully lucky today myself. A little morning shower can stir the fish up and have them looking for food. We'll get there early. Yeah, I think we'll catch something. Come on over here and wash your hands."

Josephine takes the bar of soap off the kitchen sink and gives her hands a good scrubbing. She can't figure how fish would like dough balls, but she'd take Emmett's word for it. Maybe they will catch something. She feels a little lucky herself. They get in the car and drive for a while in silence with the fishing poles sticking out the rear window of Josephine's car. Josephine usually thinks while she is driving, and foremost on her mind now is why did Emmett move into those apartments and why didn't he have enough money to pay for his groceries the other day. She couldn't ask him those things, however.

"Tell me, Emmett, do you have any family?"

"No, my wife, Louisa, died. We didn't have any children. She'd been sick a long time, and she finally gave up."

"I'm sorry."

"Oh, that's all right. I wish she'd lived, of course, but I've come to believe that there are things that are far worst than death, like being so sick and you can't get better. Louisa wasn't happy those last few years. You may not believe this, but I smiled when I saw her laying there dead. She looked just like she was asleep, peaceful like and not hurting. She lived for 60 years, and we were married for 29 of 'em. She'd be 61 now. I'm 62."

"That's nice. We're getting pretty close to the river now."

Josephine and Emmett drive on in silence, each lost in their individual thoughts, many of which hurt. But other memories lift their pain, making those hurtful memories easier to bear.

"There's a place to pull off the road over there. I've heard some say they fish from this bridge, but I'd rather find us a place down on the bank somewhere, if that's all right with you, Emmett."

"Yeah, that's fine with me. Here're the dough balls. I'll get the poles out. I don't want you to get stuck with the hooks."

Josephine takes the dough balls and picks up a small cooler in which she has packed some water, a couple of sandwiches, some chips, and two oatmeal cakes. They walk together through the tall grass to the river bank and then along the bank's edge, looking for a good place to fish.

"Right over there is probably a good spot," Emmett says. "Looks like somebody else thought so anyway; the grass is all mashed down. Want to stop there?"

"It's fine with me. I don't know anything about how to find a good place to fish. About all I remember about fishing is you have to be quiet so you don't scare the fish away. Maybe that's why I never fished much." Josephine and Emmett chuckle.

"Yeah, it's important to be quiet, as with catching anything, sometimes that's the best way, just be quiet and patient."

Emmett handles the lures carefully as he straightens out the freshly wound fishing line. Taking dough balls from the bag, he covers the hooks with dough, and gives each line a toss into the calm water. He pushes the poles into mud along the river's edge. "Now they'll stay there," he says. They sit down on some old stadium cushions Josephine keeps in her car and watch their floaters move, making tiny circles on top of the water. The ripples extend bigger and bigger until they finally disappear. Josephine notices there is about two to three feet of fog on the water as she looks across the river. It's as quiet as a lonely hillside just after fresh fallen snow. About the only sounds they hear are frogs croaking and splashing when they jump into the water. Several snake doctors fly around and occasionally land on the water along with other bugs, each making its own ripples. Tadpoles and minnows swim close to the bank where Josephine and Emmett sit. No one else is here this morning, so maybe it will be a good day for fishing. Josephine looks up into the clear blue sky and sees a lone Heron flying overhead.

Turning towards Emmett, Josephine says in a quiet voice, "I'm sorry you lost your wife, Emmett."

"Oh, well, it's tough, but about the only way to handle it is to just go on with your life, I guess. Otherwise, you'd just give up and die yourself. When I went to the funeral home to see her, she was laying there with white satin all around her. They had her all made up with her hair pulled back in its familiar club. They had given her rosy cheeks and had made her lips about the same color as the pink dress she was wearing. I looked at her and said to myself, 'She looks just like she did the day I married her.'

"For a time before she got sick, I hadn't given much thought to my feelings for Louisa. We had been married for 29 years, and would have been married for longer if she hadn't up and got sick and died. But I had taken for granted that things would always be the same. Then, when I looked into the casket and saw her laying there lifeless, it brought back memories to me of why I had married her for keeps in the first place. All our years together didn't seem like enough.

"She had worked hard right alongside me, a poor farmer. Louisa was able to stay at home almost 'til the end, only had to spend her last few days in the hospital. I talked to her then as she lay there with a blank stare in her eyes, barely breathing; her gray hair hanging below her shoulders. I kind of doubt if she knew who I was at that point or what I said, but I told her things like our life together had been good, and she didn't need to suffer any more. Somehow it made me feel better saying those things to her that I felt needed to be said. So you see, when I looked at her after that and saw that she wasn't breathing at all and was gone, I smiled to myself." Emmett's voice cracks. "What about you, Josephine, do you have any family?"

"No, well, I still have my brother, John. My parents and my sister are all dead. I never figured on getting married. Oh, I dated some when I was in high school, but I never took much of a liking to anyone in particular. The way I always figured it, why fall in love with someone who would just end up leaving you or dying on you. There's enough natural storms in life without bringing them on yourself, I always said. No, I just planned on putting my roots down deep right here, working in the store until I retire, and then building a house. But that's all changed now."

"Oh?"

"Yeah, I can't save enough money to build a house."

"What do you mean?" Emmett asks.

"Oh, it's all I can do to keep living from day to day; been working hard since high school at the store, but I can't save any money. I guess it's a good thing my parents had already died before my sister did. They would'na been able to stand it."

"Josephine, your sinker is moving. I think you got a catch."

Josephine pulls hard on her pole. Emmett reaches over and helps her. Together they pull in a good sized cat fish. Emmett carefully takes the fish off the hook, strings it on a holding line and puts the fish in the edge of the water. Then he places another dough ball over Josephine's hook, and she throws the line back into the water.

"I'm sorry for you, Josephine. That was real disappointing, I'm sure, losing your sister so young. Do you and your brother get along well?"

"Well, it's kinda funny. Things are different when you get older, of course. But, as odd as it may sound, somehow I feel all his pain. He sounded like a frightened child when he had to tell me about our sister's death. She died in a car accident a little ways past the store where I work, on her way to get something for John. I've always loved him, and he felt so guilty. I had to stick up for him, so to speak. In fact, I've stuck up for him more than once. Like the time when we were children and John killed one of our chickens. I told Mama and Daddy the dog had killed it. It was hard, though. I went home that night after he told me about her accident and cried and prayed while lying there alone. Not my sister, I prayed, not the one I had played with and loved better than myself. She was pretty as an angel. I thought about family photos that sat on tables and hung in groups on the walls. I loved her. I don't want to come close to ever losing something or someone I love ever again."

As Josephine and Emmett wait in silence for more fish to bite, Josephine's mind vividly replays another conversation with her brother.

We had a good time playing as children, didn't we, John? Do you remember how we used to skip over the roots that grew across the dirt path leading to the tobacco field?

Yeah, they're still there.

What?

The roots.

How are we going to go on without her?

I don't know. First Mama and Daddy and now her.

Josephine is silent, but her petite frame stiffens. She still remembers the feeling she had when those words of John's hit her stomach like a blow from a blunt object. The pain's not much less for her now just remembering them. Not long afterward, she noticed her hair was beginning to gray. She'd had her beautician cover it with an auburn red color. Overall, Josephine looks good for her age. She continues to be lost in her thoughts.

I don't have much savings; I used the money I got when Mama and Daddy died to put a down payment on my trailer. There is no way I can save money to build a house. I wish I could.

Scenes and words about her life keep going through Josephine's mind as she stares at the water. As was usual for her, she feels sentimental after being reminded of family. Only now, it feels different; it hurts. She misses going home and seeing everyone. Looking in the barns always brought back their own memories of romping in the straw on the floor, feeding baby calves their milk from nipples on buckets, and throwing basketballs through a barrel hoop nailed to the side of the barn. When Josephine was home, she even, at times, went into the playhouse where she had played as a child. It was a little log house, about ten feet square, where a farm hand had lived. After he moved, her father had let her play in it. Such fun she had there. And such fun she and her sister had playing with John, too. They played trucks and marbles with him. He played house and dolls with them. Life had been good while they were growing up.

Josephine rubs her forehead with her hand and slips off her plaid shirt. The sun beams brightly on them as they sit facing the east. Emmett has already shed his light jacket. To Josephine, he looks younger today; not as stooped, and the clothes he is wearing fit him better. "Here, have some water, Emmett," she says.

"I believe I will. That sun has gotten hot." Each of them drinks some of the cold water. It trickles down their throats, cooling them off and quenching their thirsts. The cold cups feel good to their hot hands. "Hey, look a there, Jose, you got another bite!"

Josephine looks up and notices her floater moving, then it goes completely under the water. "Do you think so? Well, I believe I do."

"Yeah, pull your pole up quick like you did before." Josephine grabs her pole and yanks it upward. With another jerk, she pulls the pole up higher and out of the river bank. A huge fish comes up from the water. At least it looks huge to Josephine, and it is the biggest one they've caught so far.

"Oh, Jose, you got another cat fish. Now that will make some good eating. Let me get it off the hook for you and put it here in the water with the other one."

"Whatcha gonna do with them, Emmett?"

"I'll probably eat them. I usually do. Do you like fish, Josephine?"

"Yeah, I like fish," Josephine declares. "I buy them in the store sometimes."

Josephine and Emmett fish a while longer and then eat their sandwiches. Shortly afterward the fish stop biting, and they head home with eight cat fish in all. They had thrown back several other smaller ones, along with any perch and bream they caught.

Josephine asks Emmett on the ride home if he'd like her to cook the fish for him that night.

"Why, yes, thank you. That would be nice."

When they arrive at Emmett's apartment, Josephine tells him she has a new frying pan she wants to try out so she will cook at her place. "I'll be back to get you around 6:00 p.m.," she says to Emmett. He gets out of the car and carries the fishing poles and the fish inside. That afternoon Emmett cleans the fish and puts them in a pan of salt water which he sets in the refrigerator. He gets dressed in a beige shirt and brown pants. He combs his graying hair one last time just as Josephine comes back at the stroke of 6:00 p.m. She is dressed in a blue sailcloth dress and white moccasins with small colored beads stitched on their toes. Emmett pours the salt water off the fish and puts the lid back on the pan for the trip to Josephine's. They ride in awkward silence until Josephine turns into the trailer park. "There's my place over there with the front light on."

Emmett comments on how neat it looks, with its small yard that is freshly mowed.

As soon as they walk inside, Emmett spots a checkerboard on Josephine's coffee table. It is about eighteen inches wide and three feet long.

"What a nice looking checker board. Where did you get such a thing?"

"My grandfather made it out of a piece of walnut. I don't know how he did it. How he got it that smooth and how he painted those green and white squares just perfect, I'll never know. I've looked at it and been amazed many times. The lines are straight and all the squares are the same size. He left these wide spaces on each end for the checker players to lay their extra checkers. He said he made it to play with his buddies at their neighborhood country store. They didn't have to have a table, only needed two chairs. The checker players would sit across from each other and prop the board on their knees. Do you play checkers, Emmett? You want to play a game after supper?" Josephine says as she turns the fish over to brown on the other side.

"Okay, that would be fun."

Soon Josephine puts the food on the table which she had set earlier with her mother's best blue and white dishes. "Is sweet tea okay for you, Emmett?"

"Yes, that's what I like. Sweet tea with a little ice."

They sit down and begin eating. "I always said that cat fish is the steak of fish," Emmett declares. "Look at that piece of thick white meat there on my fork. Man, is it ever good."

"Why, thank you, Emmett." Josephine, with the help of her new frying pan, had cooked the fish to a perfect golden brown. She'd also made coleslaw, hush puppies, and home made French fried potatoes. She even had stopped by the store on her way to pick up Emmett and bought a water melon for dessert. Emmett eats heartily. It is by far the best meal he's had and the best he has eaten since his wife had gotten so sick. Josephine is enjoying the meal, too. Normally, she doesn't do a lot of cooking just for herself, and it's true that working around food doesn't always set too well with her stomach.

Emmett lays his fork down and looks up at Josephine and says, "Tell me, Josephine, why do you think you never got married?"

"Oh, I told you about all of that. I just didn't want to ask for trouble. I guess I'm afraid of it, and I tell you there's another thing I'm afraid of, too. That's storms."

"Storms? I do all right in them, myself. I know we need to respect them because they are powerful and can be deadly, but I'm not really afraid of them," Emmett offers. "I do remember Hurricane Hazel, though, when she blew through back in the fifties. Louisa and I hadn't been married long then, and we crawled up under our bed during that storm. The wind from it toppled our biggest oak tree which had a trunk nearly four feet wide. The tree just missed the corner of our house when it fell. I thought about that tree last year when I had to sell the house to pay off my debts, wondered how big it would have been."

"Yeah, I remember Hazel, too. They closed the store and let us all go home when she came through here. But my fear goes back further than that, I think, to when I got caught out in a storm when I was a child. I had walked out to the woods behind our house. By the time I knew a storm was coming, it was there; and I had gone too far to go back home. Soon I felt a warm breeze as the leaves on the trees swayed gently from the passing wind. Straining to look through the trees, I caught a glimpse of the clouds. They were moving pretty fast, coming towards me from the other side of our house. That was the West side where Mama had said our biggest storms came from. As the clouds covered the sun, more darkness settled in around me. I started feeling afraid. Suddenly lightning lit up my world, followed closely by a loud thunder clap. The wind picked up its speed, making the grass along the path's edge lay over on itself. That's when I knew rain would be coming soon, and there was nothing I could do about it, maybe but pray, which I did.

"But, I knew my prayers weren't getting anywhere; I could smell rain. Soon I saw a single drop bounce in the dust, then another and another, followed by flashing bright white lightning and roaring thunder. As the first few raindrops fell and the earthy smell reached my nose, I felt big drops pelt my arms. I looked up and noticed the limbs of the old oak tree I was sitting under were too high to totally protect me in the blowing rain. As much as I was afraid to move, I knew if I didn't get under the smaller trees on the other side of the path, I would get soaking wet. I ran towards them and remember feeling the rain sting my arms with its needle-like spray. I sat down and shivered, not so much from being cold, but from being scared. I shook, and the thunder roared. Rain fell hard, but the strong tree branches, along with the huge limbs of that big oak, helped keep me dry. I sat under them, smelling the dampness in the woods and shivering. The image of being caught in that thunderstorm is etched in my memory, and I still get shaky when I see a storm coming."

"Well, you've certainly had to weather a big storm in your life, I mean with your sister dying so young and everything."

"Yeah, I guess that was a storm in a way. I did weather that storm of life, so to speak, pretty well, I guess. You've had to weather a lot, too, Emmett, what with losing your wife, I mean."

"Yes, I reckon I did. I guess we have the strength to get through what we have to. You spoke several times of praying and not feeling your prayers got very far. That's the way I felt with Louisa, just like they were hitting up against a wall. I prayed, and she got worse. But in the end, her getting worse made it easier for me to let her go. She had a strong faith. One of her favorite songs was, 'I am Satisfied with Jesus.' I wanted to have it sung at her funeral, but one of the lines says, 'Is He satisfied with me?' I didn't want to be raising any questions at that point about Louisa, so I settled on 'Amazing Grace.' I knew Louisa was in a better place. It seemed fitting that, on the Sunday following her death, we gathered at the church for her funeral. There was a power larger than life that drew her to that place every Sunday, and that song seemed fitting, too. The preacher preached a lot about sacrificing. He said some nice things about Louisa, made me feel proud. We laid her to rest in the local cemetery under some large oak trees, reminded me of the ones in our yard, which was fitting, too, I think.

"Several days after Louisa's funeral, I looked through some of her things. Everything in the house looked like her, the table by the window with the radio on it, the round pole she used to smooth the covers on our bed, the homemade straw broom standing in the corner of the kitchen, the wood cook stove, everything. The hardest thing for me was when I found her black pocketbook. I had looked in the wardrobe to see her church dresses and her black hat when I saw the pocketbook. She always took that pocketbook when our neighbor picked us up for church. She would have brushed her long hair, platted it, wrapped it in several circles and put large bobby pins in it at the back of her head. Her face would look freshly scrubbed with no makeup. She would be wearing one of her church dresses, her black hat, thick brown hose, black tie-up shoes, and, of course, that black pocketbook would be swinging on her arm.

"When we had been married for twenty-five years, she wore a dark blue dress with silver dots to church, and I had on a gray suit. I got her a corsage of pink roses, and I wore a single rose on my coat. Lots of folks congratulated us and wished us many more happy years together. She only lived for four more years. I couldn't bring myself to look in her pocketbook when I found it. It was so much a part of her. Fact is, I just got around to looking in it last night when I finished unpacking my things. You won't believe this, but I found money in it. Not a lot, but a little over fifteen hundred dollars that she had saved over the years. It was like she knew she was going first, so she saved some of her egg and butter money for me to have after she was gone.

"Times were hard for us, just as it was for many. We struggled to make payments on our home. But how we had enjoyed living there, swingin' in the homemade glider and in the hammock, and sittin' under the oak trees, eating home grown melons. I cried and talked to Louisa out loud after I found that money last night. 'You could have bought new things,' I said. 'You didn't have to cup your hand behind your ear to hear the preacher. You didn't have to tie a string around the broken end of your glasses and loop it around your ear.'"

"I'm sorry, Emmett."

"Oh, that's all right. With all that I said last night, I feel I fully laid Louisa to rest in my mind."

"Well, good. Maybe now things will be better for you. I'll straighten up these dishes, and then let's get on with that game of checkers we mentioned earlier."

"Okay, I'll help you clean things up."

Josephine and Emmett put the food away and straighten up the table. A dishwasher came with Josephine's trailer. She wouldn't have bought one out right, but now she is glad she doesn't have to hand wash all these dirty dishes. She wants to get on with playing checkers. "Here is the box of checkers, Emmett. You want to set them up while I put these dishes in the dishwasher? We can put the board on the kitchen table. I'll take this table cloth off and lay it back on the washing machine."

"Oh, okay," Emmett says as he lifts up the lid of the cigar box. Inside he finds round black and beige ceramic checkers with ripples around them. He has never seen checkers that were so nice. He'd seen only plastic ones with indentations of crowns on them. "Where did you get these checkers, Josephine?"

"From my grandfather, too. He gave them to me along with the checkerboard."

"Well, they are fine checkers," Emmett says as he moves the board to the kitchen table. He puts the black checkers on the green squares on one side of the checkerboard and the beige checkers on the other side's green squares. When Josephine finishes with the dishes, Emmett pulls out a chair for her.

They have a good time playing checkers. Once, when Emmett reaches over to crown one of his kings, his hand accidentally touches Josephine's. She looks up at him, and Emmett says, "You are a pretty woman, Jose. I've enjoyed spending the day with you, fishing and now playing checkers."

"Why, thank you, Emmett. It's been fun for me, too."

While Josephine is driving Emmett home later that night, he mentions that he would like to see her again. "I know you're young and have a life of your own, but I would like to see you again; maybe I could cook something for you at my place some time."

"That would be nice, Emmett. But I'm not as young as you think."

"I'll call you later," he says.

"That would be good."

The next day at work, the store is busy, and Josephine is training another high school student.

"I'm just peaches and cream," Josephine says when a customer asks how she is feeling.

It All Adds Up

by Barbara Hatcher Shaver

I wished I had new clothes for the first day of school, but I had to wear my best old ones.

Everyone was excited to be back at school. Sarah even spoke to me. It was a good day until Mr. Harris said, "Next, fourth graders, we'll have math. Let's review multiplication."

The class sighed a dull roar, but Mr. Harris soon said, "Sh-h-h-h, be quiet. Let's get started. Morgan, what is 9x9?"

"Eighty-one."

"Good, what is 9x6, Ben?"

"Fifty-four."

"That's right. Sarah, you're next. What is 9x5?"

Sarah answered, "Nine times five is forty-five."

"That's correct!"

Oh no, I'm next, I thought, and no one has missed a problem.

"Rachel, what is 9x8?"

What is nine times eight, I thought to myself before blurting out, "Sixty-four."

I got it wrong. The class laughed, and I felt like a dunce. I wished I was smart and skinny, like Sarah. Finally, the end of the day came, and it was time to go home.

"How was school, Rachel?" Mom asked.

Bursting into tears, I said, "I'm stupid."

"You're not stupid, honey. Don't say that about yourself."

After dinner I asked Mom to help me with math, but, as usual, she was too tired from cleaning houses all day.

It was hot lying in my bed that night. How I wished our dinky apartment had air conditioning. I also wished it was the last day of school, but it was only the first.

The next morning my alarm went off way too early.

I got up feeling bad. My throat and stomach hurt, but Mom wouldn't have believed me if I had told her I was sick. I may as well get dressed and go to school, I thought. Oh no! Mom was supposed to repair this dress. I had to sit that day so the worn place on my hem wouldn't show.

When the bus arrived at school, I didn't want to get off. To top things off, Matt had said my teeth looked like a squirrel's. I hated him, too. When I got in my classroom, I started feeling sicker. Mom had told me not to say ain't, but I said it anyway, "I ain't doing math today."

"What's wrong, Rachel?" Mr. Harris said. "Why are you crying?"

"I don't feel good."

Mr. Harris felt my head and said, "Okay, go to the office and call your mother."

While sitting in the office after my phone call, I wished Mom would hurry and come. I was scared I was going to throw up. When I finally saw her coming through the door, I ran to her. We left together after she signed me out.

"What's wrong, Rachel?" Mom asked on the way home.

"I'm sick, Mom. I hurt inside."

"Tell me what's bothering you."

"Oh, Mom, I can't do math, and I don't have pretty clothes to wear to school," I sobbed. "Yesterday I got a math problem wrong, and everybody laughed at me."

Mom said soothing things to me like it would all work out.

But what could I do to make things better, to make it work out?

I thought and thought all the way home. When I was lying in bed that night, I thought about it some more. That's when the answer popped into my head. Mrs. Blake had asked me to walk her dogs over the summer, but I had stayed with my dad. Maybe Mrs. Blake still needed some help.

The next morning I felt different. I still hated math, and I still wanted new clothes, but along with all of those old feelings, I felt new inside. As soon as I got home from school, I went to see if Mrs. Blake still needed help with her dogs.

As I nervously rang her doorbell, I worried that she had changed her mind. Mrs. Blake smiled when she saw me at the door.

"Come in, Rachel. My, you've grown. Would you like some lemonade?"

"Yes, thank you." I followed her into the kitchen where she poured me a glass of lemonade. "Mrs. Blake, do you still need help walking your dogs?"

"Yes, I do. My old aching knees don't allow me to walk much. Could you walk them this afternoon when you finish your lemonade?"

I said, "Yes, I can!" And I emptied the glass in one long swallow.

Mrs. Blake took me into her laundry room. "Here," she said, "are the leashes. I'll leave the back door unlocked. Just come on in each afternoon, get the leashes, and take the dogs out. If you walk them for a half hour, I'll pay you $5.00. I've got an old watch you can use to keep track of the time."

With Mrs. Blake's watch on my wrist, I took her dogs out.

I was nervous about walking them, but Mom had said they were nice dogs. "Stop," I yelled as they jumped on me. Then, as I began to rub their ears and pat their backs, I soon found that they were just jumping up to be friendly. I timed myself while walking the dogs for 15 minutes. Then I turned around, and on my 15-minute walk back to Mrs. Blake's, I counted the sidewalk squares as we walked across them. I had walked the dogs across eighty squares in 15 minutes.

Mrs. Blake handed me a five-dollar bill before I left her house.

"Here's your pay, Rachel. Thank you."

"I'll see you tomorrow." I smiled as I hung up the leashes.

When I got home, I added 80 to 80 and got 160 sidewalk blocks that we had crossed in the thirty minutes the dogs and I had walked. The next night I added my two five dollar bills and came up with $10.00 for two day's work. After a week of walking the dogs, I had seven times $5.00 which is $35.00!

At school, multiplication started getting a little easier, too.

I always timed myself when I walked the dogs, and it was fun to count the sidewalk squares. Sometime I'd take a different route. At other times the dogs and I ran a part of the way. Once when we ran, we crossed 120 sidewalk blocks. Two times 120 is 240 blocks that we crossed going and coming. Two hundred forty minus 160 equals 80. On a day that we ran part of the way, we crossed eighty more sidewalk blocks than when we had only walked.

That Saturday, I bought a new dress at the mall with some of the money I had earned. I wore it to school on Monday. When it was time for our math drill, I had to go to the chalkboard.

"Rachel, please multiply nine times eight," Mr. Harris said.

I wrote 9x8 = 72.

"That is correct. Great job," Mr. Harris said as the lunch bell rang.

On the way to lunch, Sarah said, "I like your new dress. It looks pretty with your brown hair."

"I bought this with money I made walking my neighbor's dogs."

"Oh, how cool to buy your own clothes," Sarah answered.

Not only was it great to buy my own new clothes, but also one of the best things about shopping was checking to see that I got the right change back, like the time I bought a sweater to match my new dress.

"That will be $13.22," the store clerk said.

"Here is $15.00." I put down two bills on the counter, a five and a ten.

"Your change is $1.78."

I counted my change. When I got home, I added it to money I had saved.

Another exciting thing I learned about earning money is saving for something you really want.

"Mom, a new bicycle costs $175.00. I have $50.00 and only need $125.00 more. I think I'll be able to save enough to buy a bike."

"I know you will, Rachel," Mom declared. "I believe you will someday have a bike of your very own."

I already had the bike I wanted picked out – the pink one in Bessel's Sport Shop window.

Bringing Out the Best

by H.T. Owen

"Alberto is making faces at me!"

"Alberto is copying my paper!"

"Teacher, Alberto hasn't done his homework!"

I often recall the first year I taught school—how I looked with great expectations into the congregation that made up my fifth grade English class. Fresh out of teachers college, I didn't know that some students had no burning desire to learn a noun from a verb, how to correctly punctuate an essay, or how to speak Standard English. Certainly, I did not know that I would be the one to learn a valuable lesson before the year was over.

Alberto Jonathan Johnson stood out. With a name like that, he was hard to overlook. He seemed to exist by himself. He came to school on his own initiative, but come he did, very regularly. He did not evidence any care or support from home. His clothes were tattered and dirty, his face and hands grimy. He brought no lunch or snack, but depended on the school free lunches. If Alberto had parents, I never saw them. They remained the silent shadows of his existence.

The children often found Alberto's oily, scum-caked comb on the floor. They reacted with disgust. "Yuk, here's Alberto's old comb, Teacher."

"Alberto," I said primly, in my best schoolteacher voice, mimicking my own teachers from an earlier era, "please keep your comb in your pocket. We do not do personal grooming when we are supposed to be studying grammar."

Alberto gave his shoulders a lazy shrug, pocketed the comb and smiled sheepishly, pretending to continue his class work as the other students snickered.

Often Alberto became involved in schoolyard fights. One day a horrified girl ran to me. "Teacher, Teacher! Alberto and James are killing each other!"

I raced to the play area. "What's going on?" I screamed, wedging myself between the angry boys.

"He started it!" James yelled, thrusting an accusing finger in Alberto's smudgy face.

"Liar—I didn't neither," Alberto retorted.

"Well, I'm going to finish it," I barked. "Both of you go immediately to the principal's office. And Alberto, you must not use double negatives."

Alberto was suspended for two days for starting a fight.

There was no doubt about it—Alberto Jonathan Johnson spelled trouble. He was not always a noisy loudmouth, but a constant undercurrent of minor problems oozed from his direction like pus from a boil.

"Make Alberto stop poking me with his pencil."

"Give me that eraser, Alberto Jonathan Johnson!"

Just enough annoyances to drive an inexperienced teacher crazy. Surely, I thought, there must be a way to bring out the best in him.

One cold winter morning Alberto came to school wearing a short sleeve shirt, gauze-thin slacks, and a vinyl jacket with long sleeves that appeared melted around the wrists. I immediately deduced that the sleeves had come in contact with something very hot—probably flames when he loaded wood into a stove. I resolved, then and there, to provide Alberto with some appropriate clothes. So as not to embarrass him with an obvious handout in front of his classmates, I stashed the clothes into two grocery bags and left them in my car. At the end of class, I motioned Alberto to my desk. "My nephews had some extra clothes they can't wear anymore. I believe they'll fit you. If you'd like to try them, go by my car and get the bags out of the back seat." I gave Alberto a half wink.

There was slight evidence of a grin as Alberto fidgeted and looked down at the floor. I didn't know if he would accept the clothes, but that afternoon I saw him get on the bus, arms wrapped around the bulging bags.

All winter I smiled inwardly as I saw Alberto sporting my nephews' clothes. One day it was John's wool cap bearing the tractor logo, the next day Chad's favorite red flannel shirt, then John's faded jeans, next Chad's warm quilted coat. I never saw the jacket with the melted sleeves again.

Maybe it was partly my imagination, but I think Alberto's behavior improved a little after my secret gift. At least, there were no more fights, and the little disruptions seemed fewer. That is, until spring arrived.

One lovely Tuesday, when all living things should have been at peace, Alberto dumped the pencil sharpener shavings squarely on top of James's head.

As if the squabble that ensued weren't enough, after lunch he threw spitballs to the front of the room, narrowly missing my desk! Just as I was ready to explode and deliver a harangue he'd never forget, I noticed Alberto's clothes.

He was nattily dressed in a spanking new outfit: white shirt trimmed in red, matching red slacks with a white stripe down each leg, and glossy red high-top sneakers. His face and hands were spotless.

How could I have been too busy burying my head in a teacher's edition to notice this brand new Alberto until he started his wild pranks?

Although my mouth stood open to deliver my sermon, the words that came out surprised me.

"Alberto, what wonderful new clothes! Are they a birthday present?"

"Naw, my sister, she come down from New Jersey and give them to me." He spoke confidently in grammar that would have sent me into fits earlier.

Overcome by the dazzling outfit, I said to the class, "Let's all compliment Alberto on his nice new clothes."

A murmur of compliments rose like a morning mist, ended by a round of polite applause.

Alberto grinned, rose, gave a comical little bow, then sat. The class laughed approvingly. Soon everyone settled down to quiet work.

Thunderstruck, I understood. Alberto Jonathan Johnson, class troublemaker, needed attention. The only way he knew to get it was by causing trouble. I had been too occupied being the perfect teacher, worrying too much about filling his head with grammar, instead of realizing that he needed words of encouragement even more.

As the year wore on, I found that positive attention such as a pleasant comment or compliment often changed Alberto's behavior for the better. Following my example, the students began to praise and compliment him for little things. Remarks such as, "That's a neat shirt, Alberto," and, "Great job on your homework," worked wonders for Alberto's self esteem.

All of us reaped the benefits of Alberto's changed attitude.

And I, first year teacher, learned a valuable lesson from my student Alberto Jonathan Johnson—that sincere compliments and genuine caring go a long way in bringing out the best.

That Thirteenth Green Was Murder

by Martha H. Lester

Rainey Patrick sat at her desk located on the twelfth floor in the office suite she shared with her boss of nine years, Gregory Chamberlain. Although it was already midday and hot as blue blazes for a day in May in downtown Los Angeles, Greg, as usual, had not bothered to come in or to call regarding the business that was once again being forced upon her to handle in his absentia. Rainey gritted her teeth when the phone rang yet again, for the umpteenth time.

In between pleasant apologies extended to each caller, Rainey felt nothing but anger towards Greg's constant disinterest in his own company. Greg was young, handsome, divorced again, and very well-to-do via his family's handed-down array of fortunes, now well into their third generation. Succinctly put, Greg was a playboy. While he invariably played around with the ladies, it was she who kept the cogs of his family's business oiled and running smoothly. The successfulness of Chamberlain Realty, Inc. was Rainey, and everyone knew it was she who breathed both life and profit into the first-rate operation that it was.

As Rainey walked over to the filing cabinet in the room, she caught a glimpse of herself in the tinted glass window that overlooked an oasis-like boulevard below. A low-flying jet cast a fleeting shadow across her image as the glass pulsated from its sonic boom vibration. It was not an unattractive woman it reverberated. She could not help but notice just how much she resembled Greg's current romantic interest, as a tall, shapely brunette with smooth olive skin and innocent fawn-like brown eyes. Thinking of Carla, however, she knew any similarities ended there physically as to all the two shared in common.

Undoubtedly, though, Greg and Carla were two of a kind. As much as she had once dreamed over the years, no, she knew she would never socially fit into the Chamberlain's world. Rainey bit on her lower lip as she closed the file drawer, having retrieved the client's folder she had come for, and dismissed this thought she had no business entertaining.

Unlike Greg, who'd been reared in this affluent family since birth, Rainey had been an illegitimate child. Because her young teenage parents had never married, she'd been raised by her maternal grandmother, Nana, when her own mother had left L. A., supposedly for some promising job in New York City. As Rainey had grown older, she'd soon realized there'd never been a job. Olivia Patrick never returned for her little girl, Helen Rainier, and the occasional letters that had once come, promising her a new home with Mommy, soon faded into oblivion just as everything else Rainey had dreamed about. So, abandoned from infancy, it had been her aging Nana, the domestic-for-hire, who'd provided for them both all the years they were up against the world on the hardship side of the city.

As Rainey stood at the window looking down upon the city's sausage link-like traffic below, she realized she'd stayed at Chamberlain Realty because the position of being Greg's office manager gave her something she'd never had in her life: prestige! She worked hard, knowing the more money she made for Greg's business, the more she'd be able to fill the chasm that anesthetized her childhood memories of abandonment, hunger, loneliness, and unpopularity, all because she had simply been born poor. Oh, life was certainly unfair. This young man who owned this company didn't care an iota about it, and she, who'd grown up without anything materialistic at all, had spun years of daydreams in just finding ways to provide basic necessities for herself and her precious Nana. Oh, Chamberlain Realty was her baby, all right, and it was her answer to every lighted candle she had ever lit in prayer.

In the nine years she had worked for and known Greg, he had married and divorced three times. Rainey had literally always been that proverbial bridesmaid and never the bride. Despite an occasional dream of life as a Chamberlain, Greg had only shown actual interest in her when he was between marriages. He was now, but he'd been for some months, keeping close company with the much younger Carla Romalotti, the interim tennis instructor at Kensington Country Club, where the Chamberlain clan golfed and partied, socially.

Rainey was positive it was fast becoming more than just a casual arrangement for Greg. Carla was not only from an affluent attorney's family in her own right, but the office grapevine had it that she'd just graduated with a degree in business administration and law from UCLA. Rainey seethed to think of yet another rich soul out in the world without any need to work at all.

As Rainey walked into Greg's office to extract a document coming in on his fax machine, she frowned to ponder her last thought. Carla certainly had excellent job qualifications in business. Compared to her Associate's degree—albeit earned through great personal expense and sacrifice by attending night classes for several years after work—it didn't hold a candle to Carla's education. For the first time ever, she thought about what would become of her job if Greg married Carla and she wanted to work with him, thereby taking Rainey's place? The fax machine emitted a buzz, jolting her back to reality. She jumped and looked around nervously, though she well knew she was alone in the office today.

Removing the letter from Greg's fax machine, she started to lay it unread, as usual, on Greg's desk. A glance at it, however, was enough to catch her eye. It was from Greg's Uncle Kirk in Chicago, a man she'd met on many occasions, but one she had never particularly liked. She knew him to be a respected mentor in Greg's life, his deceased father's oldest brother. Mr. G. Hilton, the Sr., had died shortly after Rainey had joined the firm. However, Uncle Kirk had acted in an advisory capacity during the transitional phases that followed, which found Greg emerging as the now incorporated Chamberlain Realty's new president. The trouble with Uncle Kirk was that he was also Father Kirk, and while he had a glowing reputation as a wonderful parish priest in Chicago, he knew no more about the real estate business than his playboy nephew, Greg. Nevertheless, the aging priest often meddled in this business he knew nothing about, so she and the priest had seldom seen eye-to-eye on its operations. A letter from him today could only mean that he was, yet again, attempting to interfere in how Greg should be managing his company. The conniving priest had something up his robe sleeves, but what? Rainey felt herself flush as she held his letter in her hand.

Rainey had long suspected that Uncle Kirk contacted Greg often, though she didn't know how he did it since catching him in or out of the office was no easy task, even for her. Ordinarily, she was off every Wednesday, since she worked every week-end when many people were off jobs and out shopping for new homes and land buys. Today, Greg had specially requested her to come in for the morning due to his having to "take care of something," as he had put it. Uncle Kirk must've assumed she'd not be there and that Greg would be alone in the office, as she was now. More than likely, he'd hoped to avoid her knowing Greg came in Wednesdays, and she didn't. By faxing this letter today, he'd hoped to slip some scheme of his by her fail-proof scrutiny. Fretted by the very thought of his blatant sneakiness, she did a slow burn. Aloud, she said, "You'd think a priest would have higher scruples than to stoop this low, Father!" This letter now became a must-read.

"My dear Gregory,

> *The time has come for you to wake up and take on more meaningful responsibilities within both your life and my beloved brother's business. Your first step is to immediately get rid of that detestable woman you have with you! For a while now, I have expressed my feelings to you on this matter; this subject is not new to you, son. If you cannot get rid of her, then perhaps I can help remedy this situation for you from my own connections here in Chicago. (Chicago is not without its dubious reputation, you remember.) Just do it now, I must insist, for the betterment of us ALL!*

> *God's continued blessings upon you and your dear mother, Lorraine.*

> *As ever,*

> *Uncle Kirk"*

Rainey stood stoically in Greg's office with the letter trembling in her hand. Suddenly, she felt like a caged animal! That reference to Chicago meant what, that she was to become some historically infamous Mafia "hit" to make her suddenly disappear?

Tears spilled from her eyes without warning when she thought of that term he had used for her as "that detestable woman." How dare he call her that when she personally mailed to him, each quarter, his dividend earnings that were always handsome sums in ever increasing amounts, thanks to her savvy investment sense. She knew her worth; it was just too bad that a lot of the major players at Chamberlain Realty didn't. She could not imagine that all the thanks he had for her was to be disposed of like an empty Styrofoam coffee cup! She felt totally betrayed and shattered.

The ringing phone on Greg's desk made her jump and gasp aloud. She could not hide the fear and the shock in her tense hello.

"Well, hi, angel, you busy?" Of all people it was Greg.

"Busy? Who me? Why'd you think I might be busy, Greg? Yes, I've been swamped all morning with prospective clients calling here, inquiring about quotes you promised them today. But, guess who didn't even have the courtesy to leave those quotes for me? Have you any idea how much business you've probably lost for us today, Greg? I don't need you here to make those sales, but I do need the information you've given out to our clients so that we can be consistent in what we price properties to them. That's basic Real Estate 101, remember?!"

"Whoa, what bee got loose into your bonnet? I know you took care of everything just fine, hon. You always do. You're the pro, and everybody knows it. Lighten up. If those clients can find better deals elsewhere, well, then, let them! Calm down and relax. It just so happens I might have the perfect deal just for you. Looks like my timing couldn't be more perfect, in fact. I just drove Carla to the airport. She's going to be away for a while. In the meantime, I have a favor to ask, and it looks like you and I could put the answer to some good use. Do you still play golf, by chance?"

"Not lately. I work, and you play. Remember how that goes?"

"Ouch! It seems like I have just called you in the nick of time. How would you like to play a round of golf with me on Friday afternoon. Just us, now, okay?"

"Why the sudden interest in golf with me?" Rainey asked, her voice quavering now with suspicion.

"Why not with you? I told you, Carla's out of town a while. Friday is my day off, so I thought we could just kick back on the links and let the wind blow through your pretty brown tresses. Sounds like you could use the recreation, my dear, stressed out as you obviously are!"

Rainey could not believe the audacity of Greg's assessment as to what she needed. He was clueless to see her anxiety was almost always due, in part, to his gross incompetence. She always had to do his work and hers, too.

"So, you want me to take a day off so you can just be with me? First, I want to ask you exactly what days lately have you been ON? But, yes, okay, I'll go beat you on the golf course if you're determined to be a glutton for punishment. Friday, it is. Let me know the time we tee off. I have to go, Greg. The outer office phone is ringing."

"No, Rainey, let it ring! I had a favor to ask, remember? Go into my office and look in the closet to see if my good golf clubs are in there. I don't know where I put my good clubs."

"You mean, go look right now?"

"Yeah, I'll hold. I can't recall if I brought them to the office or left them at the beach house, and Donna kept them when she got that place in our divorce settlement. Nothing rings a bell, anyway, as to where I last saw them."

Rainey didn't tell Greg that she was already in his office when he called. She paused to take up some time and then loudly banged open the closet door, went into it, and called out to him from inside it. "You do have a bag of clubs in here, Greg. It's a leather tobacco brown bag. It's a pretty color, and it looks new. Are these the good ones?"

"Yeah, they'd be the ones. Thanks, Cupcake," he yelled back loudly through the receiver. "Listen, set them out and prop them up against my desk there. I'll run by some time today and get them. That's a load off my mind as it sure saves me a trip down to Donna's, not to mention having to listen to her nagging me once I'm there. Divorced people should get to be free at last from the likes of that, you agree?"

Rainey picked up the receiver from off the desk. "I don't have the slightest idea regarding anything about your less than blissful marriages, Greg. Good-bye, and don't forget to let me know the time we tee off Friday afternoon if you expect me to show up." She hung up. She wanted to get out of there. She was too unsettled now to stay another moment.

Pulling the golf bag over from the closet to the front of his desk, she propped it as he'd instructed her. Going to the closet to cut off the light, she closed the door. A loud bang caused her to almost jump out of her skin. The bag had slid from the desk and landed on the floor. Several golf balls ran askew across the shiny hardwood floor. She retrieved them and promptly began looking for the unzipped compartment from which they must've escaped. Seeing a large, half-zipped pocket on the side of the bag, she took the balls in one hand to stuff them into the opening. Two went in, but the third met with resistance. She reached in and pulled the other two out. With her free hand, she inserted her fingers into the compartment and recoiled at once when she touched something oddly cool, metallic, and cylindrical. "What in the world?" she said aloud. Putting her hand back into the pocket, this time she brought out the object she had touched. A handgun! Why on earth would Greg have a pistol in his golf bag? She stood there in stark amazement, looking at the 0.38 caliber steel gray metal pistol. Greg had no interest in hunting or target practice, nothing that had to do with a gun. She could use a gun, though. She'd taken a handgun safety class before she'd gone to her college classes at night, since she'd had to ride the subway home alone, always very late at night. Her little gun had not been any luxury back then, for each night, she had feared for her life. She flipped open the chamber and was shocked to see it loaded with six bullets. Suddenly, she had a huge revelation, and it sent her mind spinning. She started to tremble. "Oh, Greg, is this how you're planning to obey your Uncle Kirk's orders to get rid of me? Are you supposed to KILL me Friday?!" she whispered aloud into the hand that covered her mouth.

In Greg's closet had hung a red silk culotte dress with a matching headband which she had seen while looking for his golf bag: Carla's outfit. She opened the closet door and pulled that hanger out to look at the dress. The label on it showed its size to be that of her own, a 10. She folded the dress and headband over her arm and threw the padded hanger into his trash can. She took the pistol too, rushed into her office, stuffing the gun into her purse. She grabbed her car keys and fled out the door. She had to get out of this place. She had to think. She had, most of all, to go at once to see her Nana.

Rainey drove into the parking lot of the posh, ranch-style nursing facility where her Nana had been a resident for the past four years. Suffering from strokes, Mary Helen Patrick had been left a complete quadriplegic, so there had been little for Rainey to do except to place her in a long-term care facility for perpetual care her remaining years. Rainey had settled for nothing but the highest rated facility L. A. had to offer, now that she made a handsome salary and could well afford to provide only the best for the one person to whom she owed her entire existence.

Rainey reverently smoothed the bed linens of its occupant, a frail and sleeping elderly lady with wispy thin white hair. She pulled up a chair and bent over before sitting down to kiss the soft cheek of the comatose Nana.

"If only this could be different for you and me, Nana," she whispered. The tears always came, though she didn't mean them to now. She wiped them swiftly from her own cheeks as if in fear her Nana would see them and pat her on the hand as she once always did, to softly quell any of her anxieties.

"Nana, can you hear me? I hope you can. I have to believe that you can. Something terrible has happened at work, and I'd give anything if you could just tell me what to do now. I feel so cornered, and it's all so unfair. You know how hard I work to keep Greg's company going, but I am in a real dilemma now, and there is no way I'm going to let Greg do this, not just to me, but to you, too! You will be cared for, I promise you, Nana. I have money put away, and if I don't come back, Nana, you're my sole heir, and all that I have will be kept in trust for your care. I pray I will see you again soon, but if I don't..." She choked and could say no more. She stood up, kissed again the cheek of her sleeping grandmother, and walked swiftly out of the room.

On Thursday morning, Rainey arrived at the office to find a note from Greg attached to her desk calendar. She read it aloud, "Friday. Driftwood Creek Golf Course @ 2:45 p.m." He'd scratched his initials to the note. It was certainly late enough for a tee-off time, and Driftwood Creek was not the club of Greg's usual social hobnobbing by any stretch of the imagination. Leave it to him to take her off to some sleazy golf course that she'd even heard was closing down in the near future. Carla Romalotti wouldn't have been caught dead there. Just off the coastal highway, it looked rougher and more windswept than the photos of the ancient St. Andrew's course in Scotland, where the game of golf had supposedly been born. Gullies, clusters of leafless trees in varying stages of decay, and even deep ravines accented the greens with only patchy grass on them. Her last visual memory of Driftwood Creek conjured morbid thoughts. Why had he picked Driftwood Creek?

Why, indeed! Because just yesterday he'd found Father Kirk's faxed letter telling him to get rid of HER, that was why, and Driftwood Creek might prove the perfect place for that, all right. Just to be sure she wasn't letting her imagination run away from her, however, she had an idea.

Flipping through her Rolodex, she located the phone number to Kensington Country Club and dialed it. Harry Tulloh, the assistant golf pro, answered the call.

"Hi, Harry, this is Rainey Patrick. I won't keep you for one moment, but by any chance do you have any free tee-off times for tomorrow afternoon?"

"If you mean, Rainey, do I again, the answer's no. Greg called yesterday afternoon and signed you and him up for noon. Hardly an hour later, he said he was back in his office, and he called to cancel it. Don't tell me he's changed his mind again? I can see what I could do, but that fellow just needs to grow up, kiddo, you do know what I mean? How do you stand his indecisiveness, anyway? I don't know how I can rearrange the times this late for everyone else to…"

"Oh no, Harry, no! I don't need you to rearrange anyone else's time for Greg. I was just asking to find out if he's playing there, that's all. This is just a personal inquiry, so don't mention that I called if he should call you again, would you? Thanks, Harry."

"Sure, hon, fine with me. Hope to see you soon." He hung up, relieved.

Although Rainey had much to do in the office, she was mentally too upset to work. Greg obviously planned to follow his Uncle Kirk's advice. He had cancelled their previously scheduled golf game at his ritzy Kensington Club, in lieu of a much later match with her at the run down, shabby Driftwood Creek Club. She'd intercepted the faxed letter to him, and she'd found the loaded revolver in his golf bag. Fate had supplied her with all the clues regarding her future demise! She'd stay the day at work just to look routine and unsuspecting, she decided, but spend it entirely developing her master plan to thwart Greg's own, all while getting paid by him for it!

On Friday afternoon, when Rainey drove up and parked besides Greg's red Jaguar convertible in the parking lot of Driftwood Creek Golf Course, she noticed only three cars were there. Before she could get her bag of clubs out of her car's trunk, Greg magically appeared next to her in a rented golf cart.

"Well, hello there, Mademoiselle. Do I know you, you lovely thing? Wow, Rainey, you look enough like Carla in that outfit to be her twin sister! I had no idea you looked so much like her. I'm a sucker for a good looking gal in red, don't you know. Wow!" A wolf whistle accompanied his winsome boyish charm. "Hey, you think you can beat me today?" he teased, jumping out of the cart and tossing her clubs onto the back of it with his, where he secured them with an elastic cord attached to a metal clip.

"Oh yes, Greg, I'll definitely leave here a winner, all right," she said, sitting down in the seat next to him as the driver of the cart.

"Well, I certainly hope you'll think you are by the time we get to that thirteenth green, anyway. Provided, of course, I can hold you at bay till then," he laughed. "And, by the way, this is the last day anyone will ever play this course again, did you know that? They're going to tear all this down and start over with a new course next year. That's pretty symbolic for me, as well. After today, I plan to do the very same thing, begin anew and bury my past, you might say."

"You didn't sign me in, did you?" Rainey asked, oblivious to a word Greg had been saying to her.

"Heck no, you know I know better than ever sign your name to anything, my dear!" he chided. "That would be equivalent to breaking one of the Ten Commandments, wouldn't it?" He laughed. "I'll drive you back to the club house, and you can do that. Hey, bring us a Coke when you come out, will you? I forgot to get us anything to drink."

Rainey got out of the cart and went into the office. There, she changed personality altogether. She leaned on the counter and winked at the man sitting behind at a desk. "Hello, there," she cooed. "Of all the luck, wouldn't you know I'd be stuck today with that dude outside when I bet you and I could have had such a good time together, huh?"

The middle-aged man stood up, stretched taller and leaned his shoulders back at the compliment. "Well, yes, lady, I do bet we could've. Here, let me turn this register around so I can get your name now." Rainey signed the book.

"Anything else you might be needing, uh, Miss Romalotti, is it?"

"Well, yes, but make that Carla, to you, okay? And yes, uh, Don, I will be needing two of your very coldest Coke Colas to go," she said, reaching over the counter to finger the name pin attached to his faded blue knit sports shirt. "This weather lately has been unbearable for May, hasn't it?"

"Oh, yes, uh, Carla, it surely has," he said, now running to his drink box to get out two cold soft drinks for her. He wiped off the icy wet glass bottles with a towel and set them on the counter. "Anything else now for your pleasure, Miss Carla?" he grinned.

"Oh no, Don, you've been too kind as it is. Thanks, but I'll be back before you know it." Crossing the room, she stopped as she started out the door. "Till later," she smiled and blew the man a kiss. It was signature Carla, the biggest, most phony flirt in all of California, and one that no other woman could tolerate. Going to the golf cart, she handed Greg the Cokes. She got in and ordered, "Here, get going. Let's get this game over with!"

It had been quite some time since Rainey had played golf at all, but she was no worse than Greg, who was having his share of bad shots. The course was rough and the greens nearly bare in places, making for poor scores for them both. After the front nine holes, Greg asked her if she needed to stop as they neared the club house. "I don't need to stop unless you do," he said.

"No, I don't need anything, either," she replied quietly.

He picked up the score card. "Well, it looks like you have me down two strokes. As nervous as you're acting, Rainey, I'd have thought it would be the other way around. Is anything wrong? How's Mrs. Patrick? Anything new going on with her, by chance?" he asked.

"No, I'm fine. Tired, I guess, but all right. I saw Nana yesterday. No changes with her, but thanks for asking. Just go ahead, and you tee up first for a change. It seems I'm always first, so maybe this hole will change your luck."

"Oh, rest assured, my lassie, my luck is going to change today, all right. Today's going to be my lucky day; I already told you that."

On the thirteenth tee, Greg's shot veered off to the right towards what was once a grove of trees at the edge of a ravine. Flourishing kudzu vines now ran up into the naked branches, its large green leaves covering the ground and strangling the life forces out of everything that grew beneath it. "Drive the cart over here, Rainey," Greg called to her. Getting out near where he had last seen his ball go into the vines, he went around back of the cart to get an iron for his next shot, if he could find the ball. Instead of getting a club, however, he started to unzip the pocket of the golf bag where Rainey had found the revolver.

Quick as a flash, Rainey was out of the cart, too. "What are you doing in that bag, Greg!" she shouted at him. "You've already got the seven iron in your hand now. You don't need anything else!" She slapped her left hand down hard over top his right one, now buried deep inside his golf bag's compartment.

"Rainey, what the devil are you doing?! Woman, stop, you're crushing my hand! Turn me loose! Dear God, what's come over you? I was just trying to get out this…"

"This, Greg? Were you looking for this, to use to kill me out here in the middle of nowhere?!" She stood back, pointing the gun at him. "Well, I've got it now, you see, your own little loaded pistol. And, the only thing your dear Uncle Father Kirk will ever be needed for now from you will be to conduct your last rites! How dare you treat me like dirt after all I have done for you and your company. I have worked night and day like a dog for all of you, Greg, and it has been so unfair while you've been the playboy up and down this coast, throwing away the money that I made just so you could do it! You don't deserve the price of this bullet I'm going to shoot into you, but I am going to enjoy it because I will still have my job, and no one will ever know for years whatever Carla did with you. They will only know that, one day, you and that rich harlot, Carla, went out to play golf, and you didn't return. I would love to see her face when the handcuffs go on her one day. What a privilege that, with this one bullet, I will get rid of two very rich and very obnoxious people at the same time. Good-bye, Greg. Rest in peace."

"But, Rainey!" he started to protest as the gun fired. He felt a hot sting pierce deeply into his chest. "Rainey! No! I love you! I came to tell you, I do…" He slumped to the ground beside her feet. Her heart was racing like a wildfire in the Santa Ana winds. She looked around wildly to see if anyone could have heard the shot. She saw no living thing, not even a bird. She breathed deeply, but quickly grabbed Greg's ankles and pulled hard as she could to get him to the ravine's edge. Once there, she turned him over and, pushing with all her might, sent him rolling into the thick underbrush and kudzu vines that covered a vast deep crater-like area below. She unclipped a terry cloth towel from her golf bag and used it to brush away the dragged body marks that made a zig-zaggy path in the dust to the ravine. She crumbled some dried leaves over the sandy loam until it looked normal to her. Seeing nothing more out of order, she got back into the cart and drove back to the club house whispering to herself all the way, "It's almost done. Hold on, girl, hold on. Just a few minutes more."

Only one car was now in front of the club house as she drove up to her car and put her clubs and Greg's into the trunk. She wiped off his bag with his towel so she'd not leave any of her fingerprints on it, even knowing she would throw away the clubs in a dumpster going home. She kept his towel. Now, she had to go into the club house to cover up their exit.

Going into the club house, she smiled when she saw Don again behind the desk. "Oh, love, you're still here. How wonderful. I need to leave a message with you, please. My friend outside can't start his car, so he's going home with me. He has called his garage to come pick it up tomorrow, so I just wanted to tell you we have to leave it overnight. Don't worry about it because he's assuming all responsibility for its being here, all right?" She walked to the door and started to open it to go out.

"Oh, Miss Carla, I need to ask if you have just a moment, please? You seem to have such excellent taste, I'd like to ask which gift I should choose for my wife's birthday. It's right here inside the door. I won't detain you but a moment."

Rainey had no choice but to oblige the man, though she was desperate to get out and go home. Still, she couldn't risk looking suspicious. She followed Don to the door where he stepped back and let her enter first.

As the door opened, lights flashed on, and in one loud voice, a room full of Chamberlain Realty employees shouted, "Surprise! Congratulations, Rainey!" Flabbergasted, Rainey almost fell back into Don's arms.

In the middle of the large room, a fountain flowed with champagne. Balloons and banners were swinging from every rafter, nook and cranny. Music suddenly blared from a corner entertainment center, and everyone began to applaud. "Here's your Miss Carla, folks," Don smiled.

Rainey's secretary, Delores, said, "Oh no, sir, her name is Rainey, not Carla. She only looks like that Carla, but thank the Lord it all ends there, right everybody?"

The crowd broke into whistles and thunderous applause.

"Congratulations, Rainey. Okay, let us see it!" Delores chided.

"See what?" Rainey said in dazed disbelief.

"That rock on your left hand, you silly woman! Where's Greg anyway, out moving the car? We just cannot believe he finally got the nerve up to ask you to marry him. At long last, Rainey, Greg has finally seen the light to do the right thing for once in his life! He said this morning he was turning his life around. Father Kirk, I think, finally put it to him to make you his wife, or else, and give up those no count pals of his! It's high time. We can't wait to hear how shocked you were at how he proposed. He was so nervous, so scared you'd say no. Please don't tell us you really made it hard for him, did you? Come on, Rainey, tell us every little detail," Delores begged in front of them all.

The room started to spin around for Rainey as she felt colder inside than she had ever felt in her life. The ceiling lights twirled and twinkled, while the voices of the merriment and the music in the room began to get louder and louder in her head. She felt herself slipping into darkness as she began to collapse onto the floor.

Delores, Don, and several Chamberlain Realty coworkers rushed to catch her, easing her down to the floor. "Oh, Rainey, whatever happened?" Delores frantically cried in panic.

"Oh, Delores," she whispered, as the room to her began to spin into total blackness. "That thirteenth green was murder!"

139

Ephemera

by Kristi Tuck Austin

For as long as I can remember, Nanny was peculiar. She insisted on having her tall, paper lined cabinets stocked with canned peaches and tuna. Her check book, wallet, notepad, pens, and extension cords had their own sealed and labeled Ziploc bags when housed in her nightstand. The daily Metamucil had to be mixed in the same Bugs Bunny mug, which never went into the cabinets with the peaches and tuna, but sat on the yellow dish rack.

The emergency rations I can justify, peaches for carotene and tuna for protein. The assortment of Ziplocs kept the drawer tidy. I understand the Bugs mug, it was my favorite, too. All of Nanny's oddities could be rationalized by a stretch of the imagination, except for one. Inside her battered wallet, tucked into a plastic photo sleeve, was an old Bazooka Joe gum wrapper. I would often see her slipping the wrapper out of the sleeve and running her knotted fingers over its faded, wrinkled sides.

In fourth grade, gum wrapper chains were the playground pastime for the gangly and un-athletic. Ever the over achiever, I was determined to make one as long as I was tall. Nanny said I could have any wrapper in the house except the one in her wallet. When she found me hunched over the nightstand's drawer sifting through the blue and green seals, the drawer was locked every day for the next four years. Nanny would clutch the tiny gold key in her arthritic fingers and fumble until it slid into the smiling brass slot. Sometimes the unlocking would take fifteen minutes, but her proud independence would not allow aid.

Nanny was a pioneering woman in her younger days. She was one of the first to wear pants, she got a job at the bank during the war and kept it for the next 46 years, and she refused to wear a hat on Sunday because it messed up her curls. "Why go to the Sit and Curl on Saturday if I am going to cover it up on Sunday?" Nanny seldom did what was expected. She insisted that Grand-daddy wash his own grease stained overalls. He disregarded the jibes from coworkers at the service station and went on washing his clothes until the day he died. Grand-daddy was steady, but Nanny was a whirling dervish.

Nanny's reputation is revived every May when we gather behind the clapboard church, pile our paper plates full of potato salad, deviled eggs with paprika, and fried chicken, and sit to revive the memories we were too busy to discuss during the year. About the time the coconut and chocolate pies are sliced, conversation always turns to Nanny's moonshine drinking contest. During one particularly uneventful family reunion in her youth, she baited a couple of cousins with the lure of a $20 bet. Everybody climbed into their cars and headed to the farm. While the crowd of aunts, uncles, and cousins clamored around the creek, she carefully swapped water for her jug, a fact she only admitted years later. Along with the $20 she received the undying nickname Dewey.

I never knew Dewey, the ridgepole walking, motorcycle riding, jitterbug dancing Dewey. I only knew the quiet Nanny with 15 cans of tuna fish stuffed in the cabinet. Dewey was the first woman in town to get her driver's license, but by her 67th birthday, she didn't want to get into a car. She quit the bank and stayed at home all day, rocking in Grand-daddy's green rocker-recliner.

Nanny spent most of her last few months in that recliner. She would rest her silver head against the high back and stare out the window across the corn field. Her hands sat folded on the open family Bible. When the corn kernels were plump and sweet, Nanny had to go to the hospital. For three days we waited in the taupe lounge, reading the same magazines with eyes that didn't want to focus. We ate cafeteria food and delivery pizza and talked in familiar terms with relatives we hadn't seen in years. We paced the florescent halls in a trance. I was numb.

Nanny called me into her room at 6:37 am on the fourth day. She had specified, "Just my Chickadee." I paused in the door and watched her heavy, tired breathing stir her hospital gown.

"Come here, Chickadee," she opened her eyes and called.

Four steps took me across the cold linoleum and to her bedside. The crisp white sheets made the deep purple age spots stand out on her hands. For the first time, I saw her hair uncurled; her perm was almost gone, and the wavy locks lay limp against the pillow. Her body looked narrow and frail in the mechanical bed. The side rails pressed into my stomach as I leaned forward to kiss her warm cheek. Tears made the pillow edge dance, but she clenched my fingers.

"Give me my wallet. It's beside the bed."

On her rolling food tray, the brown, leather, man's wallet rested on the worn pages of the family Bible. I lifted the wallet from on top of Psalm 23. For the first time in my 14 years, I held the smooth, stained leather in my palm. I placed it in Nanny's trembling hands.

"This belonged to your grand-daddy."

I was quiet. She held out the wallet for me to see. "This was a family photo taken when your mom was eight-and-a-half." The four Williams children sat on the front steps of the shotgun house. Mom was on the far left, and the heights stair-stepped down. Nanny and Grand-daddy stood on the porch. Nanny's dark hair was pulled up, and she wore a slim skirt. Grand-daddy smiled in his Sunday suit. I smiled too.

Behind the black and white photograph was Nanny's bubble gum wrapper. She slid it from the sleeve, caressing it between her thumb and forefinger.

"I want you to have this."

"What is it?"

"Open it."

I took the paper. I didn't know why, but my hands trembled as much as Nanny's. Inside, written in smudged pencil, were the words, "I love you."

"I don't understand," I admitted.

"That is the last thing your grand-daddy wrote. He gave it to me half an hour before the accident. He was always giving me some small sign or gesture of affection." A peaceful smile lit up her face. "He was a good man. That was the last time he told me he loved me. Now I want it to be yours."

That was the last time Nanny told me she loved me. But now I have that precious reminder tucked away in my nightstand. With that tiny scrap of paper came a great deal of understanding of a loving woman. Now I share the story and the wrapper with my children, and I have a pantry of canned tuna fish and peaches.

It Burns My Heart

by D. S. Curtis

It was summertime, and the short walk from the office to the court building was almost unbearable. My shirt felt like a clammy layer of extra skin, and there were so many people rushing along the sidewalk it was almost like the whitecaps crashing in from the sea. Oh, to be out on the boat, with the salty taste of the ocean air and watching the dolphins curve in and out of the water with the waves—there was no avoiding the only possible outcome for this day. It was the day the papers were finalized that made my son legally dead.

Everything seemed to be a haze as I walked through the doors of the Courthouse, down familiar halls that my mind barely recognized. I felt like I had switched on the automatic pilot. I passed some acquaintances, and nods of the head were exchanged. The long corridors wound around the courtrooms to the Circuit Court in the rear of the building. I found myself reaching into my pocket and fiddling with his great grandfather's pocket watch, an antique heirloom that had been passed down from generation to generation. My son had given it to me for safe keeping while he was gone. I could feel the time ticking by from the old mechanical workings in the palm of my hand. His great grandfather was a bugler in the infantry during World War II. He left behind a family of six.

In the crowded courtroom, the benches were cool and smooth. The smell of worry and fear was easily recognizable. Usually, I don't have the freedom to look around at the faces in the courtroom. On this side of the bar, I saw concern on some faces, but most people just looked angry. Some seemed to be put out that they had lost a day of work, anxious to get it over with so they could continue their hectic lives.

My cell phone rang, and the sheriff gave me a warning look. I quickly reached into my pocket and turned off the phone, never even checking to see who the caller was. Emails and cell phones are now common place. A letter in the mailbox is called "snail mail," generally because it takes so long to reach its destination, whereas emails are simply a stroke of a key. Some things seemed to come easier these days, but some things are much harder.

Waiting for your name to be called is one of the most difficult things about being in court. If you're a lawyer waiting for your case to be called, you have files to go over, or consulting with your client, but today time passes slowly, and I found myself remembering the first letter we received after my son had gone away. It came with the "Holy Land" postmarked on it. He had taken a three-day pass with a group of friends, and they had decided to visit the place where Jesus had walked the Earth. It was important to him. The symbols of love, faith, hope and peace were engraved on the ring he always wore. He wrote about how he and his friends drank strong coffee at a street-side table outside of the hotel where they stayed and how they had watched the locals doing simple everyday things so close to the warfront—like a woman walking her dog and getting all tangled in the leash—how they had watched the evening sky turning purple, and how they had been mesmerized by a huge group of hungry sparrows gulping up swarms of flying insects.

The bailiff cleared his throat. He began with the same words that he said every morning court had been in session, "All rise." The judge entered the courtroom and took his seat. So many times I'd heard those words. *This isn't the first time I've sat in court for you. You needed me when you were young and you would drive too fast. You didn't need my permission to go to war. I told you not to go. I told you that you had obligations here, but like so many arguments, you had to do what you wanted. You had to go.* I tried not to think about it. We had lots of fun times, and I tried to think of those. We'd seen many things, and we'd sailed to many places we'd never gone to before. I remember how at night, under the crisp sky, we would bundle up on the deck and watch for falling stars and look at the craters on the moon. On the sea was where I told you about reading **To Kill A Mockingbird** by Harper Lee, what an impact it had on my life and how it had steered me into becoming a lawyer. *I gave you the book, and I thought it had become your dream, too, but now I see that it was my dream for my son to follow in my footsteps. It was not your dream at all.*

I tried to listen to other cases as they were heard. The judge rambled on as he often did about the responsibilities of a delinquent parent, and I think he hoped someone in the courtroom had listened. Finally, the judge called your case, and my thoughts were brought back to the task at hand. Even as I walked forward, I still felt hope. *You have always been such a treasure. No one to be discarded this easily.* The judge assigned a final date for an empty grave in the cemetery. These thoughts burn in my mind and sting my eyes. Sometimes I feel so lost, so helpless. *I must put away doubt and believe that you did what you had to do. You heard of the battle, and you did not hesitate. You had no fear. Your life was planned to be wealthy and successful. I know you thought the risk was worth it.*

The judge looked down at the papers before him. Everything was in order. He looked at me with compassion in his eyes. He told me how sorry he was, how all the nation was indebted to all these fallen men and woman. The bailiff handed me the signed papers, and in just a matter of moments, my boy was officially dead.

Walking out of the courtroom, the artificial light blended with sunlight from the windows, and I saw a painting on the wall. I'd seen it a hundred times, but today I saw it in a different way. It had a snowcapped mountain in the background beyond the trees, and it reminded me of one of his letters. In December he was in the mountains, living in tents. He wrote and said:

"My heart pounded as the lightening and thunder of missiles crashed all around us. Men with guns came up out of the mist of the mountains. The other soldiers say the dance awaits. That's what they call it here: the dance. Take one step at a time. It is like a flame that starts deep inside—protect yourself and your unit. Do the right thing. You don't have time to think about it, just do what your training tells you to do.

There will be no peace here until these peoples' leaders look in the mirror and see what greed for power has done to them and their nation. I'm here to keep our country from becoming something like what these people have become. It has got to start with someone. Why not start with me?"

We wrote and told him that his words testified to the kind of man he was.

Some hear of a battle and immediately retreat, but you had the faith to let fear go. Your life is precious, come home to the life you have left, the ship on the ocean and the course charted. We wrote to him every week.

The hustle and bustle in the hallway suddenly pulled me away from the painting. Slowly, as if my legs no longer remembered how to work, I made my way down the hall and out the first door I came to, a door that led to the first level of the parking garage. It was cool and quiet there. I followed the heavily shadowed sidewalk to get back to the office.

Not long after we had been notified that he was missing, we received other letters. Some were from his friends saying how brave he had been. Some said he let himself be captured so that they could get away. Others seem to think he never considered that he would not make it back out from the dark path up the hill. Some of the letters said that he is a hero, and that must be true from the medals that he received. Our letters were sent back in a big box marked "P.O. Box Closed." He had been captured and was now presumed dead.

I emerged from the parking garage and saw the clouds were rolling in. The color of the sky was what we call rain blue. Not a pale blue, but a bright, almost shimmering blue. It was the kind of sky where you know there will be a rainbow stretched out across the heavens after the rain that was sure to come. The "Don't Walk" sign was lit. As the "Walk" sign popped up, a wave of people crossed over from both sides of the street, everyone politely passing each other, each person intent on his or her own life, like the whitecaps pulled by the tides.

We've been patient. Many years have passed, and there has been no word. His watch still ticks the moments by, day-by-day, and his office is still the way he left it. His name is still on the door. We want to tell our son's story to all who will listen. It burns in our hearts. Not just for our son, but for all the sons and daughters who are lost. I know the pulse of their lives still ticks in the hearts of their families and friends. We believe that anything can happen. There is no peace, but there is love, faith and hope...Yes, there is still hope.

LeOmi's Solitude

by D. S. Curtis

"Moma! Moma!"

LeOmi sat up, still fighting to pull herself away from those last few seconds of the dream. Her eyes were wide open, but through the darkness, all her mind could see was the image of her mother. The curls of her long, beautiful black hair bounced against the curve of her back with every step as she walked around the corner and out of their lives. LeOmi heard the click-click-click of her mother's fancy heels.

"Moma!"

Click-click-click.

The wind had pulled the curtains out the window, but now they pushed their way into the room. The air trapped then released in one great whoosh. The cold air brushed LeOmi's damp hair back from her face and arms, briefly taking her breath away.

She waited for the sounds of footsteps.

Then she yelled towards the door, "Good, I didn't want you to come anyway." There was a time when screams from a nightmare would bring her mother running to hold and comfort her. Not any more, and her father certainly would not come to her.

He is too busy feeling sorry for himself.

In the dark, her eyes focused on the glowing clock numbers, "3:14." Then she heard the click-click-click again.

Parts of the dream were still vivid in her mind. *What a horrible dream. There was something evil. Was it a premonition of something? But—* "Oh, I can't remember." *Dreams are so stupid. I hate them! They just make me remember things I would rather forget and make me want to do things I can't do.* She picked up her pillow and threw it at the clock on the dresser.

Click-click-click. *That sound. What is it?*

She got up with the intention of closing the window—but now the breeze felt so wonderful. Click-click-click.

She leaned out the window. Her eyes searched the backyard of the parsonage to identify the reason for the sound. The wind seemed to be fighting with a large branch from the old camellia bush, thrusting it back and forth onto her mom's old Volvo station wagon.

LeOmi felt her anger grow, and she screamed, "You might as well sell that car. She's not coming back. Not this time. You know what they say. The third time's a charm. There's no way that she's coming back this time." No lights came on from any other part of the house.

Click-click-click.

Why did you leave? She nestled her chin on crossed arms.

Click-click-click.

I knew it was going to happen. It was just a matter of time. Grandmeré says you have gypsy blood. I guess that means I have gypsy blood too. Oh, why does it hurt so much?

She has ruined everything.

"She doesn't care about me anymore. So I want care about her."

The breeze blew again. This time it seemed to console her, to say—That's right, it's your choice, only you can make things turn out the way you want them to. *Is that what she was thinking when she left? She wanted to change things. Can't she see how black and evil that man's heart is?* "How could you leave with him?"

Click-click-click.

The breeze was moist from the river. The hairs on her arm stood up, making goose bumps pop out all over her arms. She lifted her arm to watch the hairs dance with the breeze. She looked beyond her arm out the window. This time she looked past the station wagon, towards the huge, old oak tree. It swayed with such grace and beauty, its leaves flashing in the moonlight. She followed the wind's invisible course past the steeple of the church toward the river. The moonlight glistened off the waves. From there she envisioned the breeze soaring toward the bay and then down to the ocean. She could almost see the swirls the wind made in the sand and the sea foam being lifted into the air. "Fun in the sun. Why would she leave this?"

Click-click-click.

It's true we don't have a lot of money to buy nice things, but money can't buy the fun we had. How many times have we gone down to the beach? Mom would say, "Pack up some towels and a book, and lets go waste the day away." Waste. Now I know the meaning of waste. She only wanted to pretend she was someone else, living a different life in those books she read."

LeOmi laid her head on the windowsill and watched. On the other side of the church, down about four blocks away, stood the Naval Hospital pointing thirteen stories straight up into the air. The hospital was always busy, and it had so many bright lights in and around it at night that you couldn't even see the stars in the sky. There was always a steady stream of cars coming and going in-to and out-of the parking lots. An ambulance turned into the parking lot from the busy street, its red lights flashing and bouncing off the buildings and the trees. LeOmi watched as it made the turn around the building toward the Emergency Entrance.

On the other side of the parking lot the old hospital still stood, a relic of the Civil War era. They say it's haunted. Ghostly women in long white confederate style dresses and frilly hats walk back and forth on the front steps while Yankee prisoner's moans come from the basement, which is where the morgue is now.

Norfolk Naval Base had been her dad's Home Port for the last 8 years. In all that time, LeOmi had never seen or heard any of those things, but her sister Ruby had certainly tried her best to trick her. "LeOmi, come and look! There's one of those ghosts." LeOmi would run to the window, and Ruby would say, "Oh, you just missed her." LeOmi tried so hard to see the specter. She could almost be convinced it was actually there, but she knew Ruby was just trying to scare her. That was a long time ago. Ruby had been gone for 6 long years now. Her older brother Jesse had been gone for 8 years. He left when LeOmi was 2. She barely knew him. He didn't spend much time at all here at home. They both tried to come home for Christmas and summer vacations, but for the last 4 years not even Ruby had made it home for the holidays. In

2 more years she would be old enough, and that couldn't be too soon. The 7th Mountain was and is "The Best." There is none better. At least she hoped she would still be accepted for enrollment. *"I hope all this stuff happening with my mom won't affect my acceptance. They might think I'm not good enough now. I'll show them. I'll do everything better than anybody. I'll show them all."*

Click-click-click.

The moon went behind a cloud. LeOmi watched as the cloud's shadow was pulled over the land, reminding her of a thick curtain closing off the moon's light.

LeOmi sneered and yelled towards her parent's room, "It's your fault you know. All of it is your fault that she left. Why couldn't you keep her here?" LeOmi's father had been a Naval Chaplain for almost 20 years. He met her mother in New Orleans just after joining the Navy. They were married, and shortly after, her brother Jesse was born. Now at 39, her father was still a very handsome man, lean and tall with well kept blonde hair and deep blue eyes, totally opposite from that man her mother had left with. Her father is slim and light where that man is broad, and everything about him is dark. *"Are you weak, and he is strong? Is that what drew her to him?"*

Click-click-click.

*Grandmeré says I look just like her. She calls me her petit replica of Yvonne. Hair black as night and eyes like jewels—"*Are my eyes like Jewels? Oh, Grandmeré, what do you know? If that's what I'm like, then that is where I'll start." The scissors were just over on the desk. With no thought of the consequences and no sense of remorse, LeOmi grabbed some of her hair and began snipping. With each cut she held the lock of hair out over the windowsill and released it—watching, fascinated as strands were caught by the breeze and carried away towards the water. She thought, *"Maybe it will make it to the beach."* LeOmi grabbed at another lock of hair—this time she cut all the way up towards her ear, and again another handful. It didn't take long. When she was done, her hair, which once reached all the way down her back, was jagged, cropped just below her ears. She didn't hear the door open, and she didn't know how long he had been there.

"I should ask what you're doing—but I see."

LeOmi turned on her father, the scissors dropping to the floor. "What do you want, to tell me what to do? Well, go away." She ran to the bed and jumped in, pulling the covers to her head.

She glared at her father. He turned and left the doorway. She heard him yell as he walked toward his room. "Well, since I can't tell you what to do, I'll send you to your precious Grandmeré. Maybe you'll listen to that wretched witch." She heard his door slam and felt what she thought was the whole house rattle. The tears started. She wiped them from her cheeks with the back of her hands with enough force to fling the tears across the room.

The last thing her mother had said to her was "You're well on your way to growing up." *What did that mean? That I don't need you anymore, or that you don't need me anymore? I sure don't feel grown-up.*

Click-click-click.

LeOmi sat up on her knees and yelled, "I won't be like her! I will not be like her!" The angry sobs came out the window, reaching the young woman sitting concealed high up in the old oak tree. From her position she saw everything. Frowning, she took out her notebook, jotted down a few words and silently stowed it away, out of sight.

* * * * *

LeOmi finds that things do not always turn out just the way that you think they should. Join her on her quest for the Seventh Mountain and all that life as a Magi could hold.

LeOmi's Solitude, *by D.S. Curtis, is a young adult novel scheduled for release in 2007. It is a companion story of* **The Seventh Mountain** *series by Gene Curtis.*

Bury the Dead

by S.M. Foran

I saw Marshall Keene standing on the peak of his roof again. It was the third night in a row. He must have had a ladder set against the side of the house, for I never saw him actually ascend, only the shadow of his frame against the sky. He wore a long raincoat which moved erratically in the wind. He was tall, appeared even taller with his legs astride the roofline, a jagged tear of black against the dusk.

Autumn had finally settled in, the air cold with a hint of rain. I stood near the back door to my house, smoking and wondering what had gotten into Marshall. I didn't think his wife knew what he was doing. She would have certainly put a stop to his making himself a spectacle. I had seen her poke her head out the back a time or two, as if looking for him, but then the head withdrew quietly, the door clicking shut, and I saw her moving about inside the house.

Marshall didn't need to fear being discovered. Mine was the only house that really provided a view, and the front street was always deserted at this time, everyone eating dinner. The only chance he might have of being betrayed was his own dog, but the dog had been blind for nearly a year. It bumped around their yard, glancing off fence boards, flower pots, the wheelbarrow. There was no way it could see Marshall, and its indiscriminate barking had long since been ignored by Marshall and his wife.

I ran into Marshall the next night at the grocery. I had popped over to pick up some shrimp for a dinner party, and there he was in the check out aisle, a loaf of bread and a carton of milk clutched tightly to his chest. He stared vacantly at the back of the next customer.

"Hullo, Marshall." I shifted the shrimp tray to one hand so I could grab one of the celebrity magazines for my wife.

He half-turned his head, but made no other move to acknowledge me.

"How're things?" Before he could answer, the line moved, and he was next to be waited on. He dropped the bread and milk into the hands of the surprised girl at the register. Then he thrust a five dollar bill at her, took the change and shoved it into his coat pocket without even glancing at it, snatched up his plastic bag of groceries and lurched for the door.

When I got home, several of the guests had already arrived. I met my wife in the kitchen and handed her the shrimp.

"What took you so long? Everybody's nearly here." She started transferring the shrimp to a glass platter.

"You know, I ran into Marshall at the store."

She arranged the shrimp in tiny neat circles around a dish of cocktail sauce.

She didn't say anything, focusing her attention on the shrimp, then the blind dog started barking next door. "I really wish they would control that dog," said my wife.

"He seemed preoccupied."

"What?" She reached across me to grab the serving forks. "Really, Richard, you're in the way. Could you go out there and be a good host? I'm almost ready."

I stepped into the front room and began handing out drinks. Walter Steinman was our guest of honor. He had several songs appearing in a new show at the theater. We drank a quick toast, then my wife appeared with the shrimp.

Later, when Walt had been convinced to sit at the piano and play something, I slipped out back, already tiring of the party. I could hear Walt playing, everybody laughing and singing along.

I didn't even have to look to know that Marshall was at his post, staring out at a horizon lost in the cool darkness. He had become one of the nighttime features, and it almost felt comfortable to have him there perched on the roof in his coat. The Keene's had lived next door for ten or twelve years. Marshall worked down at one of the city offices—Assessor's, I think. They had one daughter who had gone off to do benevolence work with the Peace Corps a year or two back. It was only Marshall, his wife, and the blind dog now.

Later that night, after the last of the guests had finally been shooed out, I slipped out the back one last time for a smoke before bed. It must have been nearly two in the morning. As I lit up, I glanced habitually up at the Keene's roof. I hardly expected Marshall to be there this late, but there he was, standing exactly as I had seen him so many times before.

As I watched, I wondered what exactly he looked at while up on the roof. You can't really see much of the city lights from this neighborhood—maybe the treetops, the gathering clouds, or just the darkness. I glanced up and was surprised to find Marshall looking down at me, the surface of his face lighter than his coat. I looked away, a little ashamed to be caught invading my neighbor's private moments. I forced my eyes to wander over the shrubs and shapes of my own yard to show that I hadn't really been watching him, then I nonchalantly glanced back at the roof. Marshall was gone. He was probably offended at my prying and had returned to the inside of his house. I took a couple of drags at my cigarette.

"I'm sorry about earlier," the voice, near to my elbow and out of the darkness, startled me, "at the store." It was Marshall.

I flicked the ash from my cigarette, trying to hide the fact that I was shaken. "Oh, that's all right," I offered.

"I haven't been myself lately." His tall shape was muffled in the coat. I could just see the light from my house reflecting in his eyes.

"Smoke?" I offered him a cigarette, then a light. He took a few puffs and just stood there, silent.

I nodded toward the door. "We had some people over tonight," I said.

"I heard music and singing." He stood quietly for a moment or two.

The silence became noticeably awkward. Then, before I could say anything else, Marshall's dog began barking from the next yard.

"Thanks for the smoke," he said, then was gone.

Several weeks passed before I thought of Marshall again, and it was only because we were having another dinner party. I had made the usual trip to the grocery for shrimp, but had not seen Marshall. In fact, I had not seen him at all for a number of days, not even at his post on the rooftop.

"I invited the Keene's," said my wife. She set the shrimp carefully in their circles, like fallen dominoes. "I thought they might want to get out."

"What do you mean?" I asked.

"With their daughter gone and all."

"Oh," I said, setting the serving forks on the edge of the platter. "She's in the Peace Corps or something, right?"

"Don't you ever pay attention, Richard?"

"Oh, sorry." I moved the forks back to the counter.

"Not the forks." My wife continued placing shrimp on the platter. "The Keene girl—" As my wife continued, Walt suddenly started at the piano, and I only caught a few words, "—accident—flood—Southeast Asia—too bad—" She gathered up the platter and swung it around into the front room.

The crisp air met me as I stepped out the back door. The night was dark, clouds hanging low, nearly touching the peaks of the roofs, and I suddenly felt like climbing up on the roof of the Keene's house, to stand and put an arm around Marshall, but as I looked up, I saw that he was not there.

Edge of Discovery

by S.M. Foran

"Perhaps I am overtired?" Francis let his legs dangle over the edge of the examining table like an oversized child, the thin layer of tissue paper crinkling loudly beneath him each time he shifted his position.

The feeling had been coming over him for weeks, a haziness of the mind that made it difficult for him to hear what others were saying, that made it nearly impossible to respond with anything but silence or a delayed witticism that had lost its effectiveness. He was like a pugilist who had been battered mercilessly about the ring and was suffering from a brain that had swelled beyond its normal size. Everything seemed to come at him from enormous distances, and his reactions were delayed and inept.

"Perhaps. Any changes to your routine? Late nights, strain at work, social life." The doctor, a dark and waspish man in his early thirties, bent his head to write a few scribbling lines on the form held tightly to his clipboard without waiting for Francis to answer.

"I'm not myself," Francis blurted. He wanted to say more, to explain the dullness in his thoughts, the difficulty he had in carrying on a conversation, the increasing pain of merely being himself.

"Here." The doctor placed a slip of paper into Francis' palm. "Try this and get some rest." The doctor turned and walked from the room without another word, leaving Francis to stare absently at the canister of cotton swabs, the biohazard receptacle, the brightly colored poster of the human digestive system.

Francis tried to awkwardly push himself off of the table without ripping the paper, but heard it tear beneath him. He felt as though everything inside him had been suddenly removed, that he had somehow been hollowed out, the cavity of his mind left with only a hungry vapor. There was nothing left but to stop by the pharmacy on his way home.

"This brings us to the question that drives the force of the novel." He glanced out over the thirty or so bowed heads. "Why is Mersault convicted?" Silence. Francis noticed that several students had their heads resting on their arms, their books balanced delicately upright in mock attention, a skill reminiscent of horses who sleep standing up, their knees locked in position to keep them from falling over. "How is this reflective of man's existential crisis?" he continued. A watery-eyed girl was staring at him. "Mersault is Camus' existential hero—"

"What's *existential* mean?" The girl had her arms crossed. Her desk was empty. She had not brought her book to class.

"We talked about existentialism yesterday." Her question should have frustrated him, but her words sounded far away, like the lulling of a distant surf. He stood as if dazed by the heat of Algerian sands, the sunlight glancing off the desktops, blinding him, and he heard himself murmuring, "Philosophy...random chaos...meaningless."

"But if it doesn't mean anything, then why write a book about it?" The girl's soft-voiced defiance managed to snap several students from their bored reveries. He saw them looking at him, and he wanted desperately to reach out across the desks, to pull them violently into the blindness of the light, let them see for themselves.

"It's merely the realization of a truth," he managed to say.

There was a sudden dulling of the afternoon sunlight, which had the effect of luring Francis into a drowsy state, and a vision unexpectedly burst upon him. The classroom transformed itself into a courtroom, the students pooled together in a crowded booth of spectators. Francis himself sat on a hard seat by the judge, an ancient man with harsh features, a long, thin beard, and a flattened brow. Francis didn't know if he was expected to give evidence, or whether he might be the one on trial. The hard stares of the people sitting in the courtroom were almost tangible to him. The pressure of their gazes seemed to push against his chest and his head, and he felt they might burrow into his brain at any moment. He recognized the flat, disinterested faces of his students in the crowd, but was surprised to see them taking furious amounts of notes on large yellow tablets of paper. Their spasms of industriousness did not seem to match the looks upon their faces, and Francis felt the color drain from his own face as he watched them. He was not so much frightened by the idea of them pointing and laughing at his discomfort, for several of them had already started to do this, but by the thought that once one of their stares had made its way past the softened layer of his skull, it would be discovered that his head was actually empty, that he was a hollow man with absolutely nothing to offer to anyone. He turned to speak to the judge, hoping that he could make at least one person understand that he did have something to offer, that he could do better. When he turned in the small, hard seat, though, he saw that the judge was fast asleep, a law book propped carefully open and resting on the surface of the desk.

Without waiting for the vision to dissolve, Francis continued his lecture with a discussion of the Arab, the trial, and Mersault's inability to connect with anything outside of the present moment. "Mersault realizes his own existential reality," he said, "There is nothing in the universe that presses the individual except the urgency of the moment. There is no meaning or purpose outside of this." Without warning, the sound of a bell pierced the air like a thin gunshot, and the students began packing up their books, shoving them into bags and gathering sweaters and coats. "Devant cette nuit chargée de signes et d'étoiles, je m'ouvrais pour la première fois à la tendre indifférence du monde," said Francis, but they were no longer listening. "Don't forget the reading for tomorrow," he added, "The Myth of Sisyphus."

Francis did not remember leaving his classroom and only realized that he had done so when he unexpectedly found himself stepping through the doorway into his house. He absently flicked on a lamp, but the motion required a tremendous amount of effort. He dropped himself into a chair, a sense of emptiness suddenly overwhelming him, his legs buckling under the weight of the day. A wrenching sob caught him unawares and throbbed dryly through him, and he pitched fitfully on the chair until an uneasy sleep settled on him.

Francis felt an unforgiving weight pressing into his chest and opened his eyes upon the yellowed slope of a steep hill. A large stone, harsh, the flint biting into his flesh, was rolling back against him. He had apparently been rolling it to the top, but did not have the strength to continue. He braced himself as best he could, dropping one knee to the clay of the slope and rolling slightly so that the stone rested on his shoulder. A steady pressure bore into the bone, until, wincing, he had to toss himself out of its path and let the stone roll down the hill to the grey flat of the valley below. He nearly cried out at the loss, his breathing tearing the air in great ragged gasps, his fingertips digging into the clay in frustration. For a moment, as he had struggled with the stone, he had sensed a brilliant burst of light cresting the ridge, like the golden eye of a god peeking over at him, then the weight of the stone had seemed to double, something other than mere gravity pressing upon it, perhaps a colossal and malicious fingertip overbalancing the rock until it was sent tumbling down the hillside. When Francis at last managed to rake his eyes back up the slope and toward the crest, he was startled to find the gigantic face of the watery-eyed girl from his class transformed into the glory of an Olympian, a wild sweep of hair haloed brilliantly around the leering flatness of a monstrous face.

The next morning Francis stumbled into the classroom, his steps weary and halting, and he barely suspected that the hours were moving at all, let alone clicking swiftly past, so that the entire day became a swelled, rushing blur of moments that led steadily to the hour of his afternoon literature class. As the time approached and the students crushed through the doorway, time suddenly slowed until Francis could hear the grinding and crunching of hourglass sands.

The students settled themselves resignedly into their seats, and since Francis suspected that none of them had actually read the assignment, he opened his copy of Camus' essays and began reading aloud, "The gods had condemned Sisyphus to ceaselessly rolling a rock to the top of a mountain, whence the stone would fall back of its own weight." As he continued, Francis glanced up from time to time and saw the attention of the students waning even more quickly than usual, their heads drooping closer and closer to the tops of their desks, thirty-odd naps in the making, the softness of his lilting voice incapable of penetrating the fog that nestled protectively round their young minds. On and on Francis read, his voice trailing away in a hushed whisper until he finally stopped. An unprecedented silence gripped the room, and Francis stood at the front of the class, his hands lowered, the book dropping awkwardly from his hand. His face took on the light of a startled awareness, as if an unseen veil had been drawn back, revealing the world to him in a frightening clarity, one that was almost painful to the senses.

He looked out over the bowed heads. "You don't know," he shouted, "You can't know—day after day—the endless futility!" Francis stood at the front of the room, his feet firmly planted beneath him, his face flushed, seemingly aware of some truth that had always somehow managed to stay hidden from him. "You silly, stupid, simpering fools!" A rage that had been bound up inside his head for years, without any means of escape, nothing upon which it could be focused, erupted now through a mouth held wide, threatening to swallow everything before it. "Blind!" Francis rammed the petulant balls of his fists into his eyes and rubbed them furiously. "Blind! Stupid! They cannot see. They cannot know. Idiot children of idiot parents! A world captive—"

A squared object suddenly launched in an awkward arc toward Francis, a copy of the class text, its pages flapping mindlessly, missing him by only a few inches. Francis did not move, however. He stood, his arms hanging down at his sides, his anger melting almost as quickly as it had risen in his throat. A moment later, a second book flew to the front of the room, then another and another, a swift volley of paper and bindings that pelted him.

Francis just looked blankly forward, smiling slightly when one of the books glanced off his forehead. He stood before them like a Medieval martyr, his eyes no longer drawn to the faces of his accusers. Without a word, Francis removed his shoes, then his socks, and he dug his toes into the carpet as if feeling the clay of a mountain that was wasted upon the sight of those who gathered before him, a vast yellowed slope that swept away, beyond the view of them all.

The Brief Bright Hour

by Sarah Tuck

Myra had been numb and unable to speak off and on since the death of Allie 72 hours ago. Jim had held her completely in his arms several times to help tears flow and then to dry them up. Three days after his mother's death, young William had sat solemnly between Myra and Jim at the funeral home for the service.

At the funeral Myra's heart beat fast, and she felt light-headed as she studied Will. She didn't want instead to study the casket of her once beautiful daughter. Will was stoic, a soldier. He didn't cry or whine. He sat straight. His blond hair was thick, his eyes bright blue. He seemed to trust his grandparents, whom he'd seen twice. He wore a sailor suit with short pants and new sandals.

The little boy accompanied his grandparents to the summertime grave where a gentle breeze flowed overhead. Here pictures were taken of them by friends.

The Rays held a luncheon at home in honor of their daughter, a feast the whole community attended. Present was country cooking: the local vegetables, the fresh cakes, peach ice cream, and the blessing by the Rev. Gates—"Bless this family all day long, through their prayers may they be strong"—a tap-dance to celebrate a woman's life. With a clear head and more thoughts coming forth, Myra talked with Will easily. He laughed brightly at this "picnic," but their time ended when the social worker came discreetly to carry him back to Bedford. Myra held him tightly and said, "You're mine. I love you. We'll be together soon." He looked up at his grand dad when he talked about fishing in Conner Creek, "where the fish are already biting." Jim held back tears as the little boy left for Bedford. He had kept his shorts and shirt clean all day, and he marched, his hand in that of the social worker, to her car. He would stay in the foster home where he'd spent two days and nights already. The Rays stood like stone as the blue compact pulled out. They knew they'd see young Will soon.

Most of the guests and friends, still in their Sunday attire, washed dishes, dried them and placed them on a table for delivery back into the neighborhood. They assured Myra and Jim that Will would be theirs to raise and love like a son. They left with smiles and promises to return.

The days melted away fairly fast. The couple was productive. They talked to Will several times on the phone—making their heaviness light again. Then one day the expected phone call came in—for a conference with the judge in Bedford County.

Jim was silly with excitement, and Myra's voice high-pitched. They made their short range plans to shut up their house for several nights. They packed their bags with apprehension and drove off.

After much angst combined with their hopes for adopting their grandson, Myra found peace when she told herself to ask God to give to Will the best life, under their roof or not, and to believe the judge's decision was the ultimate. From the car window, on route 501, they saw there, in the clearing on the right, a buck, a doe, and a fawn. Myra swallowed her tears.

NASCAR Phantom

by Sylvia Carey

"Good night, Sparky," Jet picked up the tick-tocking, tail wagging white, black and brown Jack Russell terrier and held him close to his chest.

"Can't win 'em all, Jet," Mom said as she rubbed his head and gave him a kiss goodnight. Sparky added a slurpy dog kiss. "Tomorrow will be a better day." Mom closed the door as she left the room...

Jet set Sparky on his bed and moved beside him. A large tear rolled down Jet's cheek. Sparky cocked his head and stared. He snuggled his nose on Jet's leg.

"I couldn't help it, Sparky. My go-kart spun out on the fourth turn and hit the fence. I ran good all day, then boom, into the fence. I think I'll never win a race, not like dad and Uncle Jake. Maybe I don't have what it takes to be a race car driver."

Jet settled under the sheets with Sparky next to him. His eyelids drooped, then closed completely. Night sounds wafted outside the window. Tree frogs croaked their bass notes while whippoorwills shrilled soprano tunes. The clear sky blinked with a million stars, but one, Cirrus, the Dog Star, shed a direct beam of light straight through the clouds, straight through the trees, and straight through the open window into Jet's room. The light from the star created a path to the bedroom floor and formed a stage.

Sparky lifted his head. A low growl started in the back of his throat. Jet stirred a little and reached out to quiet Sparky, all wiry and taut. Jet felt the hackles on Sparky's neck.

"What's wrong, boy?" Jet asked as he sat up and rubbed the sleep out of his eyes. Just then he saw the stream of light coming through the window. It grew brighter and brighter. Jet leaped out of bed and ran to the window. What he saw made his mouth drop wide open. The only words he could speak were a squeaky, "Sparky, come here." Sparky moved slowly across the floor, ears back, and tail down to hide behind Jet's wobbly legs.

Jet peeked over the window sill and saw the most amazing sight. A car like no other car he had ever seen sped down the shaft of light. It shimmered all silver and pearl, shifting and changing with all the colors of the rainbow. Radiating from hood to tail fenders, diamonds of light bounced from chrome and glass. Lightning bolts flashed into the atmosphere as the car raced down the beam of light into Jet's bedroom. Jet stood anchored to the floor while Sparky trembled between his feet. Arms covered his head as nanoseconds later brakes screeched to a halt exactly in the middle of the spotlight on his bedroom floor.

Slowly Jet peered over his arm. What he saw was even more astounding than before. A silver convertible shimmered in his room with a man in the driver's seat. He unfastened his harness and seat belt. Then he stretched and raised himself to sit on top of the driver's seat. Surveying the room, he saw Jet and Sparky peering at him. The driver removed his helmet. It emitted an all-clear message as a cloud of smoke evaporated into the air. At that, Sparky made a vertical jump right into Jet's arms.

The man stepped over the side of the car and stood in full view for Jet to see. His eyes burned like headlights, but his mouth stretched into a pleasant smile. The letters "NP" shone on the front of his suit. A million dots of light flickered like fireflies in the black night to form a cape. Streams of neon lights laced his racing boots. He looked right at Jet and pointed his racing gloves at him and said, "Come on over here, Jet. Where do you keep your snacks? I've had a long ride, and I'm hungry."

Jet dropped Sparky to the floor and scrambled to his sock drawer, rummaged around and found a sack filled with peanut butter, crackers and M&M's. He meekly held it out to the stranger. Sparky scampered into Jet's closet and emerged with a bone. He nudged it to the man's feet.

"Here," the man motioned as he plopped on Jet's bed. "Come sit by me." The stranger dug into Jet's sack, dipped a cracker into the peanut butter and topped it off with an M&M. He handed it to Jet, then fixed one for himself. Sparky sat on his hind legs, paws in the air.

"Who are you?" Jet asked.

Pointing to the NP on his chest, he said, "I'm the NASCAR Phantom. I'm the spirit of all the boys and girls who want to be race car drivers."

Jet blinked hard, "Does my dad know about you?"

"Yes, and your Uncle Jake, too," the Phantom answered. "I visited each of them when they were boys about your age. I heard you tonight, Jet, before you went to bed. You don't think you will ever win a race." The Phantom popped an M&M into his mouth.

All of a sudden he stood up and shouted, "PMA. You've got to have PMA if you want to be a race car driver." Startled, Jet stared as the Phantom waved his cloak. Dots of light filled the bedroom. When Jet's eyes settled, he saw his dad and Uncle Jake standing in his room dressed in their racing gear.

"Here, let your dad and Uncle Jake tell you what it's like to believe in yourself and have PMA, Positive Mental Attitude."

Bard said, "Hey, Jake. Maybe we can help Jet with this PMA thing. What does it feel like to be a race car driver?"

"Every time I step out on the track, I tell myself, 'I'm just the fastest thing you've ever seen.'" Jake points to Bard to continue.

"That streak of lightnin' you just saw was me." Bard and Jake move together.

Jet and Sparky stood glued to the floor. Bard and Jake started singing and dancing together.

"You've got no glory if you've got no wheels.

Drive and see how it feels.

Gotta keep on rollin' along.

Roll……roll…..roll…roll

Listen to them pistons moving up and down.

Hallelujah, how we love that sound.

Gotta keep on rollin' along.

Ride….ride…ride….ride

Move over man and see what you see.

Look in your rear view mirror and it won't be me.

Gotta keep on rollin' along.

Charge…..charge…..charge….charge

Is that the finish line that I see?

Crossin' over it first is me.

Drive…drive…drive…drive

This race is mine today!"

Just as quickly as it began, the Phantom waved his cloak, and Bard and Jake disappeared.

"Wow!" Jet said, "I never knew my dad and Uncle Jake could dance and sing."

The Phantom laughed, "Now come and take a ride with me. You, too, Sparky. We're going to the Milky Way."

Jet and Sparky leaped into the car. The Phantom buckled Jet into his seat, secured Sparky and put on his own harness and seat belt. "Safety first," the Phantom said. "Now hold on."

The car sped up the shaft of light straight to the Milky Way. "Eee-Haa," Jet said as they did a 360 around Mars. "This is awesome."

"We're going to do a few touch and goes, now, Jet."

The car descended swiftly and landed on the Martinsville track, then Darlington, Daytona, Big Daddy's South Boston Speedway, until they had been to all the NASCAR tracks.

"We have one more to go, Jet," the Phantom said as the car zoomed into the night. Finally the car slowed. Jet saw the Indy 500 as the car glided onto the track. They spun around the track, hugging the walls. "See the guy with the checkered flag at the finish line? Grab it when we go by and see how it feels," shouted the Phantom.

Jet reached out, grabbed the flag and hollered to the Phantom, "I'm a winner. Do a doughnut, please, just one." The Phantom spun the car in a circle, "EEE-HAA," Jet shouted. Then, quicker than quick, they roared back to the Milky Way.

*   *   *

"Time to get up, sleepy, head. Come down and get breakfast," Jet's Mom called up the staircase.

Jet sat up in bed and looked around. "Okay, Mom, be there in a minute. Sparky, what happened last night?" Sparky burrowed his head under Jet's pillow, and that was when Jet saw a silver pin shaped like the Phantom's car right on the pillow. Jet held the pin, and rubbed it on his pajama shirt to make it shiny. "Wonder where Dad and Uncle Jake keep theirs? This is our secret, isn't it, Sparky?" Sparky wagged his tail, twice.

"I'm going to be a racecar driver someday." Jet held the pin close to his heart.

Wolfbane Blues

by Wayne D. Hodge

Lewis Davis was a desperate man.

Driven haggard by solitude and hopefulness, he had arrived at this place, prepared to take this final desperate plunge at salvation. Sitting inside a white nondescript van in an underground parking lot of a high rise apartment building, he was waiting for the appearance of the one person whom he had deduced to be the solution to his three year agonizing ordeal in hell. Sitting and waiting alone—always so alone—but the isolation was almost to its end, he doggedly waited to end this incarceration.

Desperate men took desperate measures.

To make the time pass, he reviewed the items on his mental checklist to make sure that he had not overlooked any detail that might cause this episode to end in failure. He touched the handgun inside its holster, tucked underneath his left arm, underneath his jacket, comforting and reassuring. The blindfold, a black nylon sack that he planned to slip over the head, and the handcuffs lay on the bucket seat of the passenger side, waiting to be put into use at the appropriate time. He went over the rest of his list. Everything was in order. The only thing missing now was Mason Lee, but soon, very soon, Lewis would be putting a check beside that last item as well.

Six weeks of planning was about to culminate in the final solution. He had studied and observed Mason Lee religiously, until he had known the man's routine as well as he had known the back of his own hand. Tonight, the planning ended, and the plan began.

Lewis had hoped, foolishly as it had turned out, that it would not be necessary to do things in this manner. The day before, Mason Lee had been given the opportunity to control their dealings together, but the man had squandered his opportunity. Oh, yes. He had his chance. He had the ball in his own court, but had fouled and turned it over, and now Lewis intended to score. His future, as well as his sanity, depended on it.

The view from Dr. Mason Lee's office window was a big screen panoramic overview of the Golden Gate Bridge. On Tuesday and Wednesday mornings, the days that he reserved for interviewing new prospective patients, he would sit in front of this window, before his first appointment of the day, and watch the scenes of ships and boats sailing between the Pacific Ocean and San Francisco. His passion was sailing boating. But the sight of any vessel cruising the waters was calming as he daydreamed about the wind whipping through the sails and the salt water spray on his face. For twenty minutes, before beginning the parade of interviewees through his office door, he mentally prepared himself to face the hopelessly ill who were seeking the solace only he could provide.

Long ago, Mason Lee had stopped thinking of himself as a doctor. Instead, he was now, in his terms, a businessman. His major concern, profession-wise, was not the Hippocratic oath, but the pursuit of the almighty dollar. Money had paid for the fifty story office building that he owned and the other millionaire luxuries that he enjoyed, not the self-satisfaction of healing. His clients were all wealthy and well-to-do people whom he charged handsome fees for performing his miracles. The new one hundred foot yacht that he planned to take on its maiden cruise the forthcoming weekend was testament to his philosophy of good health for those who could afford it. And his palms were just itching to steer the *Sea Baby* underneath the Golden Gate Bridge and onto the high seas of the Pacific Ocean.

Twelve years ago Mason had decided to discard his family practice for a more lucrative pursuit. Certainly his two hundred thousand dollar a year practice had kept him and his family in a fine lifestyle, but now his twenty million dollar a year business enabled him to maintain a grand lifestyle that was so much more accommodating—so accommodating, in fact, now that he was divorced, he could still afford his ex-wife and their children a grand lifestyle while living the majestic life himself.

At age thirty-five, after selling his practice, he had journeyed to China to study the ancient science of acupuncture. Like a first year internist, he had studied under the scrutiny of wise and experienced practitioners, learning the subtleties and nuances of his newly chosen field. By combining his knowledge of modern western medicine and the mysteries of old world healing, he had developed his own brand of curative procedures that had produced awesome results. And he had been determined that the world would pay dearly for his knowledge.

Pay dearly was a mild term, for his rates were such that only the wealthy could afford his services. Of course the going had been slow at first, but as he had begun to prove himself, his reputation as well as his income had skyrocketed dramatically. He had become world famous. He had appeared on magazine covers, on talk shows and had several well renowned books at the top of the bestseller lists. But his major concern was his clinic on the top floor of his fifty story office building in San Francisco, the place where he performed his miracles of healing and charged his gross fees. Before he would interview any prospective client, a five thousand dollar consultation fee was paid to prevent the begging poor and the average citizen from knocking at his door. Fewer patients and higher incomes made Dr. Mason Lee a very happy man.

The intercom buzzer on his desk sounded two short bursts. That was the prearranged signal from his secretary that it was time for his first appointment. For twenty minutes, prior to his first appointment, Mason sat at the window, collecting himself until she sounded the signal, then one minute later she would lead the appointment to his office door, and the day would begin.

Reluctantly, he stood up. He stretched while watching himself in the full length mirror on the north wall. He was five-foot ten, one hundred sixty pounds, and he kept his forty-seven-year-old muscles well toned by his various aquatic activities. His sun-bleached and thinning blonde hair and his perpetual tan projected a glowing picture of health. And he felt marvelous, too, and he winked at himself in the mirror and prepared to go to work.

He tugged on the cord that drew the draperies closed across the window.

Like everything else in his life now, the entire office was of palatial dimensions, and the window encompassed most of the east wall of the lavishly decorated office. With the distraction offered by the glass concealed, Dr. Lee was prepared to begin work.

The office door cautiously opened into the room as Mason put on his best public relations smile and strode across the carpet to greet the would-be client.

A tall black man entered the office. He was fortyish, of medium build and broad shouldered. His hair was a neat cut, close to his scalp that would make him appear bald if seen from a distance. Mason noticed immediately that the man's suit, although neat and well cared for, was not of the quality that his patients characteristically wore. But the man had paid the required consultation fee and was due a listening, besides, one never knew when a sow's ear may turn out to be a silk purse.

"Good morning. Mr. Davis, is it?" Mason was positively beaming as he approached the man who seemed hesitant and unsure.

"Yes. Uh, Lewis——Lewis…uh…Davis," was the man's clumsy reply. "Good morning, doctor."

The two men met in the center of the room, and Mason offered his hand. As they shook, Mason noted tiredness and red in Lewis Davis' eyes. Obviously, this man had suffered many a sleepless night of late. Well, that's what he was here for—that is, if the price was right.

Mason offered Lewis the chair in front of his desk, then settled into his own on the other side.

"Now, Mr. Davis. Tell me about your ailment."

Lewis watched the man squirming on the chair as though he were sitting on a hot plate. Lewis Davis was obviously unaccustomed to discussing his problems with others. He needed encouragement. "I know how difficult it is sometimes to confide in others, Mr. Davis. But I am a physician, and I assure you, your privacy will be secure. I am only here to help." The man didn't seem to relax, but he did begin to speak again.

"My illness is not a common one, Dr. Lee." Lewis' speech was measured, and his voice was low. He was leaning forward, with his elbows resting on his thighs and alternately shifting his eyes from the floor to Mason's face. "In fact," Lewis continued, "I don't believe anything of this sort has ever been recorded in history. Uh—sure, myth and legend, but not real life, I'm sure." He offered Mason a weak grin, then quickly shifted his gaze to the floor again. "I suppose my case would probably make you more famous than ever. You see I—I—" Lewis held his hands, palms up, outward in a gesture of helplessness and paused in his oratory.

Mason rose from the chair and walked around his desk. His curiosity had been aroused by Lewis' words (*more famous than ever*). Perhaps this man may turn out to be a silk purse after all. He stopped directly in front of his desk and rested his butt against the desktop's edge, folded his arms across his chest and spoke to move the man along through his hesitancy. "Please continue," he said.

"Well," Lewis said, "I don't quite how to put this."

"Just say it," Mason pleaded.

Lewis, with his eyes cast upon Mason's shoelaces, murmured something unintelligible.

"What?" Mason asked. "I didn't quite hear you." He kept his arms folded, and he bent over at the waist to hear better.

"Well—" Lewis cleared his throat and spoke in more audible tones, "It all started about three years ago when I was an electronic technician working on the Alaskan Pipeline." Mason straightened up, now that Lewis was speaking more normally again, and focused his full attention on every word as Lewis continued to alternately shift his eyes from the floor to Mason's face to the floor again. "One night, while making a line pressure check, I was attacked and bitten by this—uh —animal. You see, it was a …" His voice dropped to an unintelligible murmur again.

"What did you say?" Mason asked as he bent over again, straining to hear. He was beginning to lose his patience.

Lewis stared directly into Mason's eyes and inhaled deeply. "I know how crazy and unbelievable this will sound, but I'm ready present proof, and I really don't know any other way to tell you. But the animal was a werewolf, and I've been transformed myself. Now, every full moon—" Lewis stopped in mid-sentence, choked by Mason' Lee's reaction.

At first Mason simply stared at the man, bent over at the waist with his arms folded across his chest, frozen in that position like some ridiculous looking statue. Then, as though Lewis had shaken a rattlesnake in his face, the good doctor bolted upright with a startled expression on his face. He momentarily lost his balance as his butt teetered on the edge of the desktop, and he fluttered his arms, like a bird flapping its wings, to regain his balance. A vicious sneer twisted his lips as he cautiously moved backwards around the desk, keeping his eyes on Lewis like a mouse watching a hungry cat.

"Get the hell out of my office!" The doctor spat at Lewis. "Get out, damn you!" he shouted as he pointed at the door, advancing backwards to the business side of his desk.

"But—but—" Lewis stammered. He was standing and looking pleadingly at Mason. "But, please. I came to you for help!"

"I'm not a damn psychiatrist!" Mason retorted. He had reached the other side of his desk and was frantically pulling a drawer open. Instantly a handgun appeared in his right hand. He pointed it directly at Lewis. "I said get out!"

Lewis scampered backwards, bumping into furniture, a confused expression painted on his face as the doctor aimed the gun directly at his chest. A magazine rack toppled over when his heel connected with it and spilled half a dozen medical journals onto the carpet. Finally, he reached the door, slid his hands along the plane until he located the knob. Lewis snatched the door open and stood in the open doorway for a frozen second, fixed Mason with an icy stare, then disappeared out of sight behind the closing door.

Mason continued pointing the gun at the closed door for perhaps ten seconds. Judging that the ordeal had ended, he softly placed the weapon on the desktop and was distressed to notice that his hands were trembling slightly. He went to the liquor cabinet next to the drapery-concealed window, poured himself a short scotch and gulped deeply, the liquor burned soothingly going down his throat. Refocusing on the source of his distress, he went to his desk and pressed the intercom button. His secretary answered immediately.

"Yes, sir."

"Did Lewis Davis leave?"

"Yes, sir. He seemed to be in a bit of a hurry."

"Good. Call building security and make sure he makes the street. And I don't ever want to see him in this building again. And set the rest of my appointments back thirty minutes."

"Yes—"

Mason broke the connection before she could finish her reply.

"Damn psychopath," he mumbled. That was a close call. I will have to figure out a way to screen out the crazies before they get to my office. Could have been a messy situation if he had turned violent. Damn. Hell of a way to start a day.

Pulling the cords of the draperies, he again exposed the marine view that he cherished so much. He sat down and put his feet up. A sip from his glass, then he closed his eyes and pictured himself at the helm of his brand new yacht. The episode with Lewis Davis was already pushed to the back of his mind. A stiff ocean breeze and salty sea spray filled the crevices of his brain as cool tranquility settled in.

A car, beige Volvo, slowly cruised down the aisle of neatly aligned autos where Lewis Davis has parked his van. The headlights of the Volvo had been doused because the underground parking lot was filled to overflowing with artificial light. Two people could be seen through the glare of its wide windshield. Lewis faded back into the shadowy confines of the van's interior, a camouflaging guise he had mastered well over the course of the past several years. The Volvo pulled into a space four parking places from the white van and came to rest.

A man and a woman, middle-aged, expensively dressed and obviously returning from an early evening of doing the town, got out of the car. Arm in arm, an occasional burst of giggles from her, their bodies bumping each other lightly as they walked past the van, they headed towards the elevator. The man and woman spent the time waiting for the elevator doors to open nestled together inside a passionate embraces, cuddling and necking like teenagers standing on the girl's doorstep after a Saturday night date.

Lewis' heart ached. He longed for times past. He longed for the life he had been forced to shed, the warmth, the tenderness, the woman he had shared his life with, enjoying the simple intimacies that he was now only able to witness in others. As the man and woman disappeared behind the sliding elevator doors, he stifled a sob that lodged itself inside his throat like a lump of cement, hard and unyielding, and refused to dissolve no matter how hard he swallowed. Although it had only been three years, it seemed as though he had spent his entire life deprived of the love and affection that he so desperately craved. *Desperate*—suddenly that word had become the central theme of his life in his struggle to regain his lost past and ease the pain that permeated his heart.

Lewis reached for the nylon sack on the bucket seat beside him. He found a small measure of comfort as he clutched the fabric and squeezed, wringing it in both hands as though he were wringing a wet towel, a security blanket that represented his desperate (that word again) plan for salvation.

A check of his wristwatch relayed the fact that the time was upon him. Any minute now, Mason Lee would be making his appearance. Four weeks of studying the man's routine would very shortly culminate with the initiation of Lewis' plan. He hoped to hell that he hadn't overlooked any details that might cause him to fail. No. Failure was not a thought he could afford to entertain. This venture would end successfully—all he had to do was maintain his cool and follow the procedure he had mapped out.

Of course, he felt it shouldn't have to be this way. Mason Lee didn't have to react so violently. Lewis hadn't expected the man to accept his story at face value, but he had at least expected him to have been more tolerant and given his story a listen. Certainly he hadn't expected the man to pull a gun. After all, acupuncture wasn't exactly mainstream medicine, and Lewis would have thought that someone involved in such as unorthodox science would have been more interested in what he had to say. But there's no accounting for human nature. He didn't know if Mason Lee's reaction had been anger or fear, and he really didn't care. Survival was the only human instinct he was concerned with, and his survival instincts were razor sharp right now. Lewis felt relieved that he had decided to map out this plan before going to see Mason Lee. Now it was his turn to react, and Mason Lee would discover that Lewis Davis was a desperate man and he could not be denied.

Lewis let his eyes wander among the rows of parked vehicles. Rows and rows of expensive automobile gleamed underneath the fluorescent glow of the under ground lights that cast the garage in a sea of perpetual brightness. Although the parking lot was security tested and could only be entered by inserting a coded pass card into a computer slot, breaking in had been a piece of piece cake for him. His background as an electronic technician in past times provided him with the necessary skills to infiltrate the security that the building's tenants paid so heavily to maintain. But over the past three years, he had been forced to learn many new skills in order to ensure his survival. Things that he had once considered out of the question during his past life were now ordinary and second nature to him. His self-developed skills as a thief and forger had enabled him to finance this very costly operation. After all, he couldn't very well just visit his friendly neighborhood banker and apply for a loan to finance a kidnapping and miracle cure. He was on his own, in hiding, but he had learned to cope very well. Despite the impossibility of the situation, he had learned to be a survivor.

Contact. The silver Mercedes belonging to Mason Lee was majestically cruising down the same aisle that the beige Volvo had, only moments ago, traversed. With headlights on high beam. as though it were the lead car in a New Year's Day parade, the Mercedes crept slowly past the back of the van, inching its way towards the elevator doors. The glass was tinted so that it was impossible to see inside to know the identity of the Mercedes' passengers. He had observed this scene enough times to know that Mason Lee, his fourteen-year-old daughter, and twelve-year-old son were the only passengers.

Per routine, Mason Lee had spent Thursday evening with his kids, dinner at a fashionable restaurant, private time at his home then returning them to their mother. Every Thursday the man performed his dutiful divorced fatherly duties. Lewis grunted with disgust at the thought; Mason Lee took for granted what Lewis Davis considered precious.

The silver Mercedes came to a stop directly in front of the elevator doors, creating its own parking space. The threesome slid out of the Mercedes and headed for the elevator. Mason walked with his arms around his kids, and the threesome appeared as the picture of familial normalcy as they boarded the elevator and disappeared behind the sliding doors. All per routine—Lewis knew it well.

Lewis breathed a heavy sigh of despair.

The longing in his heart strangling and suffocating. In another time and in another life, Lewis had been a father (two sons), a husband and a very happy man. But life had canceled his prescription. Happiness was now a distant memory on a distant plane.

Alaska. At the time, it had seemed like a good idea. A bounty of opportunity just waiting for the eager and adventurous, and for Lewis Davis, a good opportunity was what he had needed most.

Lewis has been an electronic technician with a wife, who worked as a secretary, and two elementary-school-aged sons. Their combined income had been enough to adequately support the family, few frills, but it had been enough for an average family, living an average life in Norfolk, Virginia.

Then came the dread of every working person in America—layoffs. Lewis' eleven year tenure with Atlantic Coast Electronics, Inc. had ended abruptly. The company's major bulk of work had been with U.S. Navy contracts, and due to cuts in

U.S. military spending, the result was much less work for civilian technicians. Lewis' salary had been two thirds of his family's income, and the sudden loss had been devastating, to say the least. Of course there had been unemployment benefits, but it had not been nearly enough, and the package was only temporary. An alternative had been sought.

Lewis had picked up the pamphlet at the local state employment office while there filing his employment claim, three weeks into his jobless state. Tacked onto the wall, beside the bulletin board where job openings and employment laws were displayed, had been a box filled with the pamphlets proclaiming the desperate need for qualified personnel to fill out the workforce required for the continued smooth operation of the completed Alaskan pipeline. His job skill had been listed among the required, and the pay scale was enormous. As he delved deeper into the information pamphlet, his mind kept wandering back to what the money and the numerous advantages could afford his family—perhaps the layoff had been a blessing in disguise. New hope beamed on the horizon. This opportunity had been too good to pass up— no matter how far the journey.

In three weeks time, Lewis had his bags packed and his plane ticket in his hand. Standing in the airport terminal with his wife and two sons huddled close besides him, he savored the comforting presence of their closeness, a comfort he would be denied while the kids finished out the school term and Lewis secured lodgings for the entire family in Alaska. The disadvantages were all negated, Lewis and his wife had agreed, by the financial benefits of the move to Alaska. All was bright in the Davis family's future as Lewis had boarded the plane and waved a fond parting to his loved ones standing at the air terminal windows.

Lewis had smoothly settled into the routine of his new life. He had been assigned as part of the maintenance crew deployed to maintain the pumping and monitoring stations at optimum operating condition, a crew of technicians and operators that maintained a twenty-four hour vigil. Except for the abundance of nearby white iced landscape and cooler temperatures, the living had not been much different than what he had been accustomed to back in Virginia. He had snugly settled in and prepared for the forthcoming arrival of his family. Everything was going to be okay.

Three weeks before the planned arrival of his family, the bottom fell out of Lewis Davis' basket of contentment, and his life was transformed into a never-ending horror show.

Two to three days of snow and wind had been forecast for the end of the week. All necessary scheduled outdoor work that could be accomplished before the end of the week had to be pushed ahead and tackled by all available hands. On Tuesday, Lewis, Carl, and Ed had donned their parkas and set out on snowmobiles at seven o'clock that morning to perform stress tests on a section of pipeline where pressure readings had been suddenly fluctuating. The work had been slow and time consuming, and eventually the three men had realized that, in order to complete their task, they would require an additional hour of work past the scheduled time to start heading back to the base. Half of the return trip would be after dark, and after conferring briefly with their supervisor over short wave radio, it had been agreed upon by all that it would be best to complete the work now instead of returning in the morning.

The bright cloudless sky had gradually transformed into a star-filled vast panoramic scene of beauty as the three men had snowmobiled across the frozen plain towards their home-base. The moon, two days from being full, had been a round quiescent observer casting its cool illumination glow upon the icy landscape as Lewis admired its luminous and mysterious beauty. He had reveled in the cool onrushing air that brushed against the face and the quiet confident hum of the engine beneath him as he and his two companions had motored home. Lewis thought that, at last, he had found happiness, and soon the crowning touch would be the arrival of his family. Life was grand—full steam ahead.

The three men were guiding the snowmobiles in a tight formation, with Lewis in the middle and his companions on each side of him. No one had noticed the snow white four-legged creature, the size of a newborn colt, that had streaked across the frozen terrain to the left and slightly behind them until it had been too late—much—much—too late.

When it had come within three feet of the traveling trio, the creature had launched into a powerful leap; barely brushing across Ed's forehead, continuing onward into the left side of Lewis' head and knocking him off his snowmobile onto the frozen ground and finally landing on Carl's back, biting deeply into the right side of his neck with long exposed fangs and dragging the helpless man onto the frozen ground.

Momentarily disoriented, Lewis had clumsily clambered to his feet, regained his senses and took stock of the situation. The two unoccupied snowmobiles were still traveling onward, unattended. Ed was turning his mobile around in a wide arc, headed back in their direction, and the animal had poor Carl pinned to the ground with its forepaws, savagely attacking the man's now exposed neck. Carl's arms and legs were flailing helplessly while he screamed his last agonizing dying breath, his blood tinting the frozen white ground around his head deathly red. Lewis started toward the animal, waving his arms and hollering at the top of his lungs, trying to distract it from poor Carl. The animal ceased its attack on Carl immediately and sailed toward Lewis.

Lewis' first impression when the animal had snapped its head around and looked in his direction was that it was a gigantic white dog, a monstrous canine from hell with Carl's blood dripping from its frosty snout. Then, as the animal had leaped at him, instant recognition had dawned. It was a wolf, the biggest damn wolf probably on the face of the earth. Lewis brought his right forearm upward in self defense as he stumbled backwards and fell flat on his back.

The wolf's powerful jaws clamped down on the sleeved arm, and Lewis screamed in agony as he felt the bone break in two places. He attempted to ward off the attack with his awkward left arm, while the vicious jaws attempted to get at his throat. He could hear the teeth clacking together at each failed attempt. The wolf's foul breath fumed into Lewis's face, its eyes wild and savage, blazed with bloodthirsty fury. Distantly, somewhere behind the pain and turmoil inside his brain, Lewis had heard the sound of rifle fire that was ignored by the attacking beast. The savage jaws changed tactics and tore at his shoulders, shredding the parka and tasting the hot flesh and blood underneath. Then it was at his chest and at his stomach, the snapping jaws inflicting awesome pain, and Lewis was beginning to feel his resistance failing.

Another rifle shot, and the wolf had yelped once and rolled over twice away from its victim. It lay still for a moment, then surprisingly regained its feet and agilely bounded away across the barren frozen landscape.

Lewis lay helpless on the hard snow-packed ground; the pain from his ragged wounds tortured his ravaged nerve endings to the edge of endurance, while his own life's blood seeped into the frozen snow. Through the fog of pain and anxiety, he looked at Carl's prone and motionless body lying thirty yards from him, the blood coloring a wide circular pattern around his head and shoulders, and Lewis knew that his new found friend had seen his last sunrise. Then, Lewis was aware of Ed kneeling and bending over him, checking his wounds and trying to comfort his ailing comrade with news of help being on the way—and to just relax. Relax? Lewis tried to laugh, but could only manage a weak grimace. How the hell could he relax when his wounds felt as though they were on fire and his blood was leaking from his body? Relax. Shit. And silent hot tears streamed from the corners of his eyes, not from the pain of his wounds, but from the pain in his heart as intuited with a great degree of certainty that he would never again share the loving comfort of his wife and children. And eventually, as sweet and painless unconsciousness lay claim to his pain ravaged mind, Lewis was grateful.

During the six weeks of planning, Lewis had clocked Mason Lee's best time at six minutes for the round trip from his car to dropping his kids on their mother's doorstep and back to his car again. Six minutes was all the time Lewis had given himself to be ready for the good doctor's return. Six minutes was more than enough time. He would be ready.

The instant that the elevator doors had closed, Lewis eased into action. He hastily stuffed the handcuffs and nylon sack into the pockets of the sports jacket that he had slipped on to conceal the gun and holster strapped to his upper body, then got out of the van and calmly walked towards Dr. Lee's Mercedes, attempting to appear inconspicuous in case someone should appear inside the garage before the caper was complete. He tried the driver's side door. Locked. Never fear, he possessed his own set of keys. Lewis quickly unlocked the door, slid in behind the steering wheel and started the engine. He parked the car in the nearest empty parking space and relocked the door before walking away.

The elevator shaft was a ten foot by ten foot square steel column that ascended impressively and disappeared into the high ceiling of the underground parking lot. The shaft was at least fifteen feet clear of the wall behind it, where Lewis planned to duck out of sight in case of any unexpected arrivals. Lewis positioned himself to the left of the elevator doors where he was easily concealed by the shaft's sharp corner. He was now within grabbing distance of anyone exiting the elevator doors, as well as being unnoticeable to anyone leaving the elevator, particularly someone shocked by the unexpected absence of his Mercedes.

Lewis cautiously scanned the parking lot. He didn't expect to see anyone else down here; there was very little or no traffic through the building at this time of the evening. No security guards were employed. This was an ideal setting for a kidnapping. He checked his watch; seven minutes had passed, and Lewis was poised to pounce.

At the ping of the elevator doors, Lewis's muscles involuntarily tensed like a leopard on a tree limb poised for the attack. Mason Lee stepped into view, he stagger-stepped as his mouth gaped open at the unexpected absence of his car. "What the hell is...?" Mason exclaimed aloud, then snapped his moth shut as Lewis pressed the point of the gun barrel into his ribs and remained behind him, out of sight. Mason's hands instantly began reaching for the sky as the word *robbery* undoubtedly filled his mind.

"Put your hands down, Doc," Lewis said.

Mason did as he was told. "My wallet is in the breast pocket inside my jacket," Mason said quickly.

"I don't want your money, Doc. Just walk straight ahead to that white van. Move." Lewis pushed the gun barrel against Mason's ribs for dramatic effect, and Mason responded immediately. The two walked in tandem with quick strides to the side of the van. "Stop," Lewis commanded when they had reached the van's sliding side door. "Grab the handle and slide the door open." Then another poke in the ribs.

"Who are you? What do you want?" Mason questioned as the door slid smoothly to the right on well oiled tracks.

"Plenty of time to talk later," Lewis responded and roughly shoved Mason between the shoulder blades until he was face down on the van's thickly carpeted floor, his feet still flat footed on the ground. Then, moving like a rodeo cowboy roping a calf, Lewis grabbed and jerked Mason's wrist behind his back and slapped cuffs on in record time. Suddenly Lewis heard the unexpected smooth purring of an expensive automobile approaching from the opposite side of the garage.

"Hey, take it..." Mason began his plea.

"Shut up," Lewis hissed as he climbed onto Mason's back and whipped the nylon sack down over the good doctor's head, and collecting his hostage by the back of his belt, he gave a healthy tug and rolled into the interior of the van, pulling Mason along and depositing him in the middle of the floor like a bundle of rage. Then Lewis clambered across Mason's body, grabbed the door handle and slammed it shut. He heard the car's engine shut down a few feet from their position and voices as the occupants unloaded. Lewis warned Mason, "One peep out of you, Doc, and you're dead." Mason didn't respond—he only lay motionless, huddled on the floor with his hands cuffed behind his back and his head completely covered with the hood. Both men held their positions in silence as the unseen people passed the back of the van and disappeared behind the elevator doors.

"Okay, Doc, lets roll," Lewis said as he crawled between the bucket seats in the front and climbed behind the steering wheel. He started the engine, backed out of the parking space and nonchalantly cruised towards the garage entrance. "I'll take the blindfold off and make you more comfortable when we're clear of the city. But, right now, I need you quiet and humble." Mason's only response was his heavy breathing beneath the nylon sack. Lewis took a good look at the man to judge that his bull-like panting wasn't anything health threatening, then shrugged off his apprehension and concentrated on making his escape.

Lewis silently congratulated himself. So far his plan had unfolded without a hitch. As he drove through a quiet San Francisco suburb and the bright city lights began to fade, he was beginning to feel more at ease with each mile he covered and was beginning to think that perhaps his situation wasn't so desperate after all. He cast a quick glance into the back of the van where Mason Lee was captive. The man had sat upright some time ago and was now resting with his back against the wall. The good doctor hadn't attempted to communicate at all since their journey had begun. His silence was totally unexpected. Lewis had anticipated Mason to be kicking and screaming all the way. That was just the picture Lewis had held of Mason Lee in his mind, a rich bag of wind, soft with life. However, Lewis didn't know if the man was paralyzed with fear or had simply conceded to his fate. Or perhaps Mason Lee was slyly biding his time for the right opportunity for a revolt. Lewis reminded himself to remain cautious. But, actually, either way it didn't matter, as long as he had the doctor under his thumb, everything would be all right.

Finally, away from the population of prying eyes, Lewis pulled the van over onto the side of the road. He figured it to be safe enough to unmask his traveling companion and make his journey more comfortable. He flipped the switch for the interior lights and crawled into the back of the van.

"Okay, Doc. Time to uncover." Then he pulled the nylon sack up and off his hostage's head.

Mason breathed a deep sigh, blinked reflexively and stared maliciously at his captor.

"If looks could kill, Doc, I would definitely be a goner," Lewis casually remarked.

"I should have guessed," Mason sighed. "Who else would be crazy enough to pull a stunt like this. Unfortunately, for me, I didn't pull the trigger back in my office when I had the chance."

Lewis released a huge burst of laughter, and he instantly felt his tension evaporate. Now he knew where he stood. Mason Lee was full of fire and was not a man to be taken lightly.

"Doc! You surprise me. I didn't think you had so much fire. Yeah, you're the right man for the job all right."

"I don't know what the hell you're talking about. What damn job?" Mason replied, full of belligerence.

"I'll explain. But, first, let's get moving again," Lewis said. He motioned Mason towards the passenger side bucket seat with a palms-up gesture of his left hand, while assisting with a firm grip on Mason's left bicep with his right hand. After the doctor had awkwardly struggled into the passenger seat, Lewis slid into the driver's seat and unholstered his revolver. "Okay, Doc. Twist around so I can uncuff you." Mason eagerly presented his backside, and Lewis deftly inserted the key into the left cuff, and the mechanism released with an audible click.

Mason pulled his arms forward and stretched to ease the stiffness. Then, as though he had remembered that he had turned his back to a rattlesnake, he snapped his head around to stare at the grinning Lewis Davis.

"Feels good, hey?" Lewis said. Pointing the gun at the doctor's chest, he said, "Now cuff the open end of those bracelets to that iron bar on the side of your seat."

Mason didn't respond. He only continued to stare at his captor.

"You know, Doc, if you're considering trying me, that would be a grave mistake. I'll put a bullet in your chest before you get your arms raised. Now why don't you do as you're told, and let's get this show on the road." The point of the gun barrel never wavered from its target.

Moving with deliberate slowness, the doctor found the iron bar that Lewis had welded onto the metal frame at the bottom of the bucket seat. Using both hands he snapped the handcuff shut around the bar and sat back, staring directly ahead through the windshield. The left hand was free, but the right hand was restrained and confined him to the boundaries of the bucket seat, neatly imprisoned.

Convinced that his prisoner was firmly in place, Lewis reholstered the revolver. He started the engine and pulled back on the road to continue their journey. Along a two-lane blacktop that wound its way into California foothills, they continued to put distance between themselves and the San Francisco metropolis. Away from the saddening crowds and bustling traffic, the journey carried them deeper into rural northern California and closer to Lewis Davis's moment of salvation.

"Where are we going?" Mason finally asked after half an hour of silence.

Lewis glanced at the doctor, was silent for a moment, then decided the time was right. He turned on the overhead light. "Okay, Doc. Despite what you think, I'm not crazy. No. Not at all. Although, in the beginning, it was much easier for me to believe myself over the edge than to accept the reality of this nightmare I've been living for the past three years."

"Your—werewolf problems," Mason stated. He looked out the side glass. "So now you've pulled me in. Deciding to share your madness."

Lewis did not reply. He reached forward and opened the glove compartment on the dash. He pulled out a sheaf of newspaper clippings stapled together and handed them to Mason. "Here," he said, "take these."

Mason looked at the paper in the outstretched hand momentarily, then hesitantly reached for the offered packet with his free left hand. "What's this? Proof of your madness?" he wise-cracked.

"Go ahead, read," Lewis said, "Keep you from getting bored."

Mason breathed a heavy sigh of resignation and begun thumbing through the clippings. Lewis noticed from the corner of his eye that the good doctor's interest had piqued as he advanced to each succeeding page.

"Now that I think of it," Mason said, " I remember this. Yes. Alaska. National news. Quite a stir as I recall. Three men attacked by some kind of animal while returning from a work assignment." He flipped to another clipping. His eyes widened, and he looked directly at Lewis for the first time since riding in the front seat. "Well, no questions about it. This news photo is of you all right. But this doesn't prove your sanity—only that you've suffered through a serious trauma. As a matter of fact, now that my memory has been jogged, I seem to remember that you disappeared from the hospital. A large scale man hunt was mounted, but the patient was never found." The doctor grew silent while he read. Quietly, with his eyes still downcast on the clippings, he said, "Just my luck you had to walk into my life. At the hospital people died ghastly deaths. Tremendous property damage. Wild stories surfaced, but no satisfactory answers." Finally he looked at Lewis directly again and exclaimed, "What the hell happened there?"

In less than fifteen minutes, the rescue helicopter had located and collected Lewis and his co-workers and was whisking them away to the hospital. Lewis had remained unconscious and was hovering on the brink of extinction. Carl was pronounced dead on the flight back. A stunned and uncommunicative Ed, physically unscathed by the ordeal, sat against the copter's bulkhead, his eyes riveted on his fallen comrades as the emergency medics labored in their efforts to perform their magic.

At the hospital, the doctors and nurses had been waiting, and they instantly took command of the situation. Carl was dead, that was certain, but Lewis had a chance, and the miracle workers wheeled him away to surgery. Eight hours on the operating table, and the miracle workers had decreed that they had done their best. Now the rest was up to God as the patient was wheeled into a recovery room. The death watch had commenced.

The story had hit the news wires, and a media sensation had been created. The eyes of a nation were focused on the perils of Ed, Lewis and Carl. The faces of the family members were televised, tormented and teary eyed, across the nation.

Every newspaper in the country had run the story on page one. A room at the hospital was set up to accommodate the press. Suddenly the death watch was nationwide.

Thursday afternoon, two days after Lewis and his two co-workers had snowmobiled into tragic infamy, the weather arrived. The predicted snow storm had come barreling into town. The entire area had suddenly become blitzed with winds and snow that had paralyzed the movements of the entire city. Anyone who had not been prepared had suddenly run out of time.

Inside the hospital, Lewis remained comatose in his bed. The death watch continued.

Sometime around midnight on that Thursday night, while the snow was steadily piling up outdoors and the winds were savagely blasting against the windows, the ruckus began. A nurse making her rounds was walking down a lonely corridor when an agonized male scream echoed off the walls. She raced down the hall and stopped, three doors up from Lewis Davis's room, where she heard the unmistakable sound of glass shattering. She boldly pushed the door open, and what she had seen caused her to turn as pale as the white uniform she wore. The patient assigned to this room lay sprawled, face up, across the bed; his left arm had been torn off completely from his shoulder, his throat and chest were ripped open all the way down to his navel. The monitoring equipment had been over turned and smashed as well as the glass in the window where the howling wind was pushing the snow into the room by the shovelfuls. But the two-legged creature she had seen standing there in the middle of the room with its fangs and claws dripping blood forced a milk curdling scream from the bowels of her being and sent her stumbling down the corridor, proclaiming hysterically that the minions of hell had been unleashed.

Patients' doors began opening to investigate the commotion, but closing immediately in panic at the sight of the gruesome, hairy manlike creature that was swiftly following the screaming nurse down the hallway.

Hospital staffers and patients alike quickly converged to investigate the source of the commotion. Then their own screams of panic reverberated when they had seen the ungodly horror in hot pursuit of the screaming and fleeing nurse. A mad scramble then ensued for the nearest exit, laundry chute, closet or any other vehicle of escape or camouflage that had been immediately available. The panic was so complete that several slower moving recuperating patients were trampled, and one orderly even ran blindly into a wall and knocked himself unconscious. The creature easily overtook the panicky retreaters, grabbed one doctor by the seat of the pants and shirt collar simultaneously, raised the poor fellow over its head and tossed him into the fleeing herd. Like bowling pins, the frightened throng toppled over, rolling and sliding across the highly polished tiled floors, screaming and moaning in panicked agony. A primal howl of victory, bellowed by the creature, filled the corridor as it beat its fists heavily against its hairy chest, and it briefly surveyed its handiwork then quickly trotted away in the opposite direction, turned a corner and disappeared from sight.

For the better part of an hour, the creature had roamed the hallways, slipping from floor to floor, taking on all challenges and repeatedly demonstrating its physical superiority. By the time the police could maneuver through the blinding snowstorm and arrive to the rescue, the creature had found its way to the ground floor and smashed through the glass doors of the hospital's front entrance to escape into the blizzard, never to be seen or heard of again.

In the aftermath, eleven people had been discovered dead. Thirty-seven had been reported wounded, and one person was unaccounted for—Lewis Davis. No trace of the comatose patient was ever discovered, and because of the disheveled condition of his room, it was safely and wisely assumed that the creature had either devoured or carried the poor man away into the night...no other explanation was acceptable.

The deathwatch had ended.

Mason Lee opened his eyes. A brief moment of disorientation passed as he scanned the walls of the unfamiliar room and remembered how he had come to be there. He tried to sit up, but this movement was restricted by the handcuffs tying his right wrist to the metal rail of the bedspring. He looked to his right and saw that the other bed was empty. Lewis was already up and about —damn that maniac. Mason realized that he was in a precariously dangerous situation, dealing with a madman, and that his life was in serious jeopardy. That fool actually believed himself to be a werewolf, and Mason realized that his chances of survival were slim now that he was an unwilling participant in Lewis Davis' insane illusion.

Mason decided that his best course of action was to follow Lewis's lead and wait for the first opportunity to get the upper hand. After all, how could someone so obviously insane continue to hold the reins so steady much longer? Mason looked across the room to the door of the bedroom. All he could do right now was wait for the madman to reappear.

They had driven all night, sticking mainly to secondary and occasionally a back road or two. After leaving the San Francisco area, Mason had no idea at all where they were. Lewis had been extremely clever at disguising their destination, and the only thing Mason knew for sure was that they had finally driven up into the mountains, but what mountain or what state was a mystery to him. All through the ride, Lewis had narrated his life after the attack in Alaska, giving details of all he perceived to be truths, truths that Mason had continued to silently pass off as a madman's delusions, and increasingly enforcing his belief that in Lewis Davis he was dealing with a major nutcase. Mason had read and reread the newspaper articles about the catastrophe, had listened and listened to Lewis' explanations, had concentrated to remember all that he could about his own impressions at that particular time in history and had finally concluded that Lewis Davis' explanation didn't even remotely coincide with a rational train of thought, and so decided that anyone who could give credence to such a story was not a well person. And in Mason Lee's tide of rationality, as with any sane person, werewolves were just myths and fairytales. So Mason had decided to neither humor nor rebuff this madman; instead he only listened and plotted an overthrow. But the opportunity to seize control of the situation had never occurred as Lewis had remained equally cautious throughout the night, even during their brief rest stops. And Mason was thoroughly dumbfounded at how the inept and fumbling Lewis Davis who had sat in his office could handle this kidnapping with calm and cool confidence and skill, but he was also thoroughly convinced that the calm and cool would snap at some point and he would be able to take command quite easily. Thus Mason had been forced to continually remind himself to be patient, and he would be home in time to take his new yacht on its maiden cruise as planned. Eventually they had arrived at their destination, a rather pleasant two-story mountain cabin somewhere in a wooded and isolated area (only Lewis and God knew where), shortly after sunrise. After several more hours of weak apologies and reminiscing about life in Alaska, they had settled down in a bedroom with twin beds and gone to sleep, weary from the night long journey.

Mason heard footsteps on the stairway outside the bedroom, a pause, then the door swung open.

"Ahh! Good morning, Doc." Lewis stood in the doorway, grinning from ear to ear like he was on vacation at a mountain resort. "Well — actually it's not morning," Lewis continued chirping as he entered the room and approached the bed where Mason lay, "But you get the idea. Hey?"

"What time is it?" Mason asked.

"A little after five. It'll be dark soon, so we had best get a move on." Lewis unholstered the revolver again, then reached into his jean pocket and retrieved the handcuff key. He tossed it onto the bed beside Mason. "Unlock yourself from the bed and recuff both wrists."

Then he backed off to a safe distance and watched.

Damn, Mason thought, the lunatic was still being extra cautious. He did as he was told, then he sat on the edge of the bed waiting further instructions.

"Okay, come on, let's go," Lewis commanded as he gave instructions by pointing the nose of the revolver in the direction that he wanted his captive to go.

Lewis allowed Mason to use the bathroom (a bathroom which had been thoroughly stripped bare of anything that could be used as a weapon) and wash up while keeping a safe nonconfrontational distance. They went downstairs to the kitchen where sandwiches and coffee were waiting. Lewis continued to keep his distance, the revolver forever ready to be used as a club or for firing. All the while, Lewis continued to talk, eternally expressing his confidence in the good doctor and how he had been looking forward to this time for so long, even occasionally apologizing for putting the doctor through this inconvenience, but constantly assuring that it would be well worth the effort. All the while, Mason watched and plotted—one mistake was all he needed, just one mistake.

Mason wasn't sure how long they had sat at the kitchen table drinking coffee, but he soon began to realize that nightfall was rapidly approaching. As the light began fading, so did Lewis' good humor, and he began taking on a more somber attitude.

"Okay, Doc. It's time," Lewis said. And he pointed the nose of the gun in the direction for Mason to lead.

"Time for what?" Mason asked as he got to his feet. He still wasn't quite sure what was expected of him. Nothing was clear except that Lewis Davis was insane and dangerous.

"Time to get the show on the road," Lewis replied. His face was void of his good humor and the earlier cheer.

With his hands cuffed in front of his body, Mason led the way down the flight of stairs that began in the back of the kitchen. The stairway descended into the basement. At the foot of the stairs was a short walk space and an open doorway. Mason entered a large room with dark wood-paneled walls that were devoid of any windows or wall ornaments. Lewis followed close behind.

"Okay, Doc. This is your new clinic. For the time being anyway," Lewis said as he closed the door. The door was at least six inches thick and made of some type of heavy metal. Lewis grunted slightly as he pushed the door shut with some apparent effort and then spun a wheel attached to the center of it like a roulette wheel.

The door reminded Mason of a bank vault door. He remained silent and watched Lewis work.

"This door is controlled by an electronic time lock," Lewis said. "I installed the door myself and rigged up the timer." He pointed to a round-faced electric clock mounted directly over the door. "We're locked in until eight o'clock in the morning—well after sunrise. So you've got all night to do your thing."

"Which is?" Mason asked.

"Like I said, to cure me," Lewis answered. "I know you can do it, Doc." He walked to the center of the room and stood beside a raised concrete platform with a bare mattress lying on top and steel shackles strategically positioned for feet and hands. "Go ahead. Look around, Doc. I've got everything you need here. My medical files, x-rays, electronic monitoring equipment that I don't know jack shit about, but I'm sure you do, and—oh, yes—the essential tools of your trade, your acupuncture needles. I've got it all fixed up for you." He gestured with an open palm, inviting Mason to investigate the equipment.

Mason walked around the room, his back to Lewis, examining all that had been laid out. He was impressed. Despite the man's madness, he had done a rather remarkable job of equipping the lab—certainly not fully equipped, but enough for him to "do his thing," as Lewis would say. Mason thumbed through the file of x-rays and selected an appropriate film. He posted it on the illuminator and flicked the light switch. He had selected an x-ray of Lewis' skull and posted two more of his brain. He examined, but was disappointed when he didn't find any evidence of brain tumors, lesions or anything else that might cause odd behavior. He turned away and stopped mid-step when he saw Lewis. The fool had climbed onto the mattress and had fastened the shackles onto his ankles and wrists, and a heavy chain had been secured across his chest. Mason breathed a heavy sigh of relief. The lunatic had finally made a mistake.

"You seem to have made yourself comfortable," Mason said as he walked towards the restrained Lewis Davis. The tension was gone from his voice, and for the first time since this ordeal had begun, he felt he could relax.

"A necessary precaution, Doc. After all, after I change, you can't work on me if I'm busy tearing your throat out." Lewis had his eyes closed and was breathing deeply. "It won't be long now. I can feel the change beginning deep inside of me. It must be dark outside. I can always tell."

"Lewis. Where's the key to these handcuffs?" Mason asked hopefully. "I need my hands free so I can work." Work on getting out of here, he thought.

"Look on the gurney behind you."

Mason spun on his heels and spotted the key lying on top of a shiny metal hospital table with wheels. He eagerly marched to the gurney that was bare on top except for the key. His elation caused him to fumble momentarily, but he succeeded in releasing the cuffs and threw them onto the cement floor, uttering a grunt of disgust. Now, to find a way out. Totally ignoring the imprisoned Lewis Davis, he headed for the door. He grabbed the wheel attached to the center of the door and unsuccessfully attempted to turn it until he was red in the face. He examined the door's edge, but discovered, much to his chagrin, that the seal was too tight to attempt prying it open. The door was airtight and impenetrable. Okay, so I'll have to find another way out, he thought.

"Help—me—Doc."

A cold chill crept up Mason Lee's spinal cord. He froze, insensibly afraid to turn around. The voice that had pleaded for help was guttural and soulfully lost. The air was suddenly charged with an electric tension. Something phenomenal was happening.

"Help—me—Pleassse."

Mason broke the paralysis by jerking his body around to face the pleading man. His jaw went slack, and his heart skipped a beat. A nervous perspiration broke out on his forehead. He rubbed his eyes with the heels of his hands. This can't be happening, he thought, now he's drawn me into his delusion. But Mason knew this was no illusion; his basic instincts told him so.

A short, but coarse layer of hair was beginning to grow on Lewis Davis' forehead, and his jaw and chin were beginning to protrude slightly, but noticeably. His hands jerked inside the shackles, and Mason became aware of patches of hair growing on the backs of the man's hands.

Mason approached cautiously. Too stunned to think, he simply continued to stare, slack jawed. Lewis opened his eyes and looked at the doctor. "Helpp meee..." he pleaded. His voice was becoming gruffer and gravelly. "Pleassee."

Mason checked the shackles to be sure they were secure, then he gingerly touched the man's forehead which was beginning to protrude before his very eyes, and the hair was becoming longer and thicker. Now, instead of words, a low growl escaped Lewis's lips, lips which were becoming thinner and parting to reveal elongating teeth that would eventually become fangs. Then, unexpectedly, the changeling snarled viscously and snapped his teeth at him. Mason, startled into retreat, gasped and stumbled backwards.

Sudden panic filled Mason's head. He thought about the hospital in Alaska and the dead, and he was instantly certain that his own life was in immediate danger. He frantically looked around for the revolver. Where'd he put that thing? The snarling was more persistent now, and Mason looked at the thing and saw the cold primal viciousness in those eyes, and his panic escalated.

He made a mad dash for the table with the acupuncture needles and grabbed a handful. He cautiously approached the thing that wasn't Lewis Davis anymore. The face was three quarters covered with a thick matting of hair, as well as the hands. The facial features were more canine than human. Growling and snarling, with saliva drooling from the corners of it mouth, the creature was straining to escape its bondage. The restraints held steady, and Mason stopped at the platform's edge, poised to plunge three microscopic sharp acupuncture needles into the beast's heart.

"Wait!" Mason spoke aloud. " I'm being so damn stupid." Here he had the opportunity for unprecedented greatness, and the only thing he could think was to kill the beast. "A damn werewolf," he whispered with wonder in his voice. He checked the restraints to be sure they were still holding fast, then held a single needle in his hand while transferring the others onto the edge of the mattress. First thing, tranquilize. The bold and brash Mason Lee resurfaced as he cautiously inserted the needle into the proper point at the juncture of shoulder and neck to connect with the proper nerve, while the werewolf strained unsuccessfully to pivot its head enough to take a bite of the offending fingers. The beast instantly ceased its squirming and visibly calmed as the needle was further inserted to its proper depth. Mason smiled as he mentally patted himself on the back. Another needle carefully inserted into the shoulder on the opposite side of the body and—walla! The creature closed its eyes and began a deep sleep, breathing deeply and evenly.

Mason was beside himself with pride and joy. Dr. Mason Antoine Lee—werewolf tamer. He burst into a gala of laughter that bounced off the walls of the basement room like echoes in a carnival fun house, but the creature remained undisturbed, trapped inside its deep slumber. Gradually Mason got his joy under control and checked his needle insertions—firmly in place and operating at peak efficiency. He had to admit to himself that he was quite a genius. Mason had never admitted to himself that he was quite a genius. Mason had never known such fulfillment before. This was his greatest moment.

The patient appeared to be resting comfortably. Mason gave Lewis a tender pat on the thigh—and to think I called you crazy. Despite the new found affection he felt for Lewis Davis, or the creature lying unconscious before him, Mason still felt a wave of revulsion at the physical ugliness of the werewolf. He turned his back and rested his haunches against the edge of the make shift bed, preferring the blank view offered by the far wall rather than the gruesome sight of the monstrosity asleep on the mattress. Now I have better than twelve hours to kill before eight o'clock and the timer releases the lock on the door. In the morning, I'll get us back to San Francisco. From now on, I'll run the show. I'll probably hold a press conference over the weekend to unveil my latest triumph and maybe—yes!—hold the press conference aboard my yacht. This is getting good.

But for the time being, he would find some constructive use of his time while confined inside this dungeon. He let his eyes wander among the equipment Lewis had assembled for his use. But it was no good. His thoughts strayed back to the triumph of the moment. He attempted to contain the case of the giggles that suddenly erupted, but the feelings were too good, and he gave in to the moment. Hey, the money I'll make from the book alone will be a king's ransom. Perhaps I'll be generous and share with my old buddy Lewis, here—but—then again—HELL, NO. And suddenly a fresh burst of giggles erupted. He was like a six year old locked inside a candy store after all the grownups had gone home.

But his joy evaporated instantly as the sound of metal stretching and tearing pierced through the fog of his happiness-clouded brain. And fear, cold and numbing, crept up his spine like icy marauding fingers as he realized the werewolf was breaking free.

NONFICTION

Academics Aside

by Margaret S. Covington

(This is part of a series of stories written about my experiences in first grade with my "dreadful" teacher, Miss Smith. In hindsight, she was one of the strongest teachers I encountered, and she was possibly exceptional.)

In the 1950's public schools weren't meant for everybody. Although I preferred not to go, I wondered what happened to those who weren't allowed to stay. It did not take long to distinguish between the two options, and I found it troubling to think about for very long. Miss Smith had several children in her care who had problems to deal with that simply would not go away. It didn't seem right to me that life was not balanced on equal scales. My naive perspective of the world was changing.

In our class, one table seemed to be the harbor for the misfits who couldn't behave. They were spaced between well mannered children made brave through the ill fate of having to sit there. At that particular table sat three students I will long remember, Sammy, Beverly and Billie. They lived on "Doodle Hill," a part of town on the north side commonly referred to as "The Hill."

Sammy

Rowdy Sammy, ruffian that he was, resembled a flat-headed circus monkey in railroad-striped bib overalls. Typically Sammy popped out of his seat and pranced around his area of the room. He was forever pulling braided pigtails, snatching paper and pencils from startled neighbors, or thumping someone's head. He thought nothing of elbowing anybody close by saying, "Watch this!"

"Watch this!" became a signal for such antics as simultaneously dropping several marbles on the floor just to see them roll to the wall. Swallowing pennies in a gulp or two was another of his distractions. One of his irresistible pranks was slipping a chair away from an unsuspecting girl after reciting the Pledge of Allegiance, thus causing her to tumble to the floor and cry. At that point he would caw like a crow. He didn't mean any serious harm, but Miss Smith didn't care. She seemed to pull a ruler out of thin air and whack his palm a few times with such force the snarl on her angry face would frighten the dickens out of the rest of us. After Sammy yowled a few times, he slouched back to his seat, snickering, "She can't hurt me, she can't hurt me." As long as I stayed out of his way, I thought I could get used to that little devil. There was no way I ever wanted to be anywhere near him, so I would haughtily bustle by him with pursed lips and scornful eyes, catching him in the periphery of my vision. Whenever I had to brush by him (mind you, at the farthest distance possible), I cradled my possessions close to my chest and stuffed my scaredy cat side in the pit of my stomach in hopes it would not escape.

One time I had to venture near his table to get a box of crayons, and I heard that cawing voice call, "Who 'er you?"

I froze.

"You heard me, who 'er you?" he insisted.

It scared me so badly that my mouth dropped open like Jonah's whale. I turned to him with my hand on my hip, declaring, "It's none of your business who I am, leave me alone."

He didn't stop.

"Who 'er you?"

"I'm not telling you who I am. I'm getting a box of crayons."

Joel, one of the wise guys at his table, muttered across the table, "Leave her alone. Margaret's bigger than you."

A split second later, Sammy laughed and sprung back," What are you going to do, sit on me, (pause) Margaret?"

I was ready to wage war with the wise guy who muttered my name, yet scared to death of that bibbed primate, Sammy. Joel was protected by Sammy. He was no dummy. Joel figured out how to rescue a potential enemy…think for them and tell them what they wanted to know. He was guarded for life. I was ready to murder Joel at that point, and I hated what Sammy had just told me. I wished I could just sit on him and squish him through that clunky chair. I glared at him with the meanest face I could make, trying to think of a mean thing to say and not get hurt. However my scaredy cat side started escaping. I realized I was up against a brain and a dangerous goofball, so I marched myself back to my seat with crayons in hand, dismissing them both, thinking, "Boys are so dumb…why do they have to pick, pick, pick all the time?"

With a flick of my hand to brush the hair out of my face, I flipped that problem aside. It was easy to do at age six. I had learned a lesson in choosing my battles, and two against one was just not a fair fight. I knew, if it kept on, all three of us would have our hands popped by that awful ruler, and I would probably cry. I was scared of Sammy, all right, but he wasn't as mean as that teacher. It's best just to draw a pretty picture and color it brightly.

After that incident, Sammy left me alone; I was of no interest to him thank goodness.

However, all of us had to deal with him on his good days and terrible days. Then he got sick. He started breaking out and clawing his arms and legs all the time. It bothered Miss Smith, and she tried to get someone to take him to the local health department. That didn't happen right away. Eventually he developed so many open sores and purple boils topped with pus that Aunt Ruth, our principal, came to our class to take him away. He wasn't allowed to stay in school for a while when that happened, impetigo was contagious.

When he did return, Miss Smith had to treat those places with special ointment so they would go away. Sammy had to go away a few more times during the year when his behavior was too much for Miss Smith and the rest of us. After those episodes, he always came back to school, grinning with his innocent looking eyes roosting over his broad monkey grin. At six I didn't consider that his life was full of serious problems generated from living on "The Hill." I only understood that he was one of those stupid troublemakers you didn't mess with at all costs. That was what I needed to know about Sammy. At the end of the year, Sammy did not have "promoted to the second grade" written on his blue report card. Maybe life was balanced, after all, just in a strange way.

Beverly

Beverly took on a feline appearance with her thick mane of tangled hair. When the school year started, she mumbled more than she talked and flailed her arms wildly if someone set her off. Beverly came to school in dull colored plaid dresses with lopsided hems. If they had not popped off, cheap metal buttons fastened some of her dresses together. Early in the year, I thought Beverly was slammed into a large cage when she got home…a cage for wild humans seemed like a feasible option to me for someone as wild and out of control as she appeared to be. Like Sammy, she lived on "The Hill" and probably scratched around for everything she had. At times Beverly was too ornery to be happy and too desperate to care. At other times, she said funny things and laughed as loudly as country folks do when "rocked back" in ladder back chairs around pot bellied stoves in general stores.

Soon after Sammy had to leave school with impetigo, she had to leave, too. When the sores started planning their attack, her mouth was the bull's eye they hit. The sight of those crusty sores formed on her lips and face made it very difficult to go near her at any juncture of the day. The people from the Hill were not the kind of people you fooled with, unless you grew up with street smarts administered by the grace of God at birth.

Beverly didn't stay away long. She returned to her seat at the end of that special table. She didn't seem to care that she was at the "bad" table and was regarded much like an untouchable by most of the class. It could have been that she wasn't going to know that since no one was going to tell her. I could not understand how she could be so bold in the face of adversity. There must have been some secret ideas she had learned about people that she used favorably. I wished I knew them, but that was not for me to know. Beverly was determined to be included in anything she deemed important. Maybe her scrappiness came from living "on the Hill." Beverly knew how to push herself forward as if a large hand invisibly swept her wherever she wanted to be. If she was bothered by what others said to her, she never let it show; she wasn't concerned about people's perception of who she was. Beverly would walk right up to people and make herself important when she clearly was not. She stayed around when we were rude beyond reproach: she came along when we deliberately left her out. Beverly got in line near us, and we hated her for doing so. Whenever this outcast was around us, we pulled our dresses in close, so as not to be contaminated. It was like us to scrunch close together so she couldn't get near. But she was there. Beverly even had to eat lunch with us sometimes. When the lunch room food was good, it didn't matter who you were if you had something somebody else wanted. No good food was forbidden food, just coveted when not your own.

After I realized that Beverly wasn't going to just go away, I was more tolerant of her and her misfortunes. She sat across from me one sunny day in the lunch room when the menu included hamburgers, French fries and canned fruit. After I gobbled down my French fries and mustard slathered hamburger, I was ready for more. Beverly had not touched her fries. I was willing to wager she had not breathed on them either, since they were on the far side of her tray. Therefore, they were safe for consumption.

"If you don't want your French fries, I'll take them," I volunteered. Some of my friends looked at me like I was crazy, eating off of Beverly's tray. They were speechless.

"You can have them," she said and shoved her yellow tray near my blue tray. This malnourished girl had eaten her fruit and most of her hamburger, but the fries were all crispy and untouched. After a quick perusal of her food, I "whipped" her fries onto my tray with delicate finger sweeps and looked at her with "new eyes." There wasn't a vacant look or a wild look in her eyes, just blue-green eyes like an Asian tigress. They might even be pretty if she wasn't sad. She didn't smile, and she didn't say much more. In this cold mode of communication, I figured she didn't care about me any more than I cared about her. She had something I wanted, and I was willing to risk getting every last French fry.

"Thanks, Beverly."

I grinned and poured ketchup all over the fries and treasured each crispy bite. Did I think to offer her my fruit? I did not and instinctively knew she would never, ever ask for it. Besides, I might have wanted it before we left the lunch room. I had no reason to share; it was more pleasurable to get what I wanted without the pain of giving something up. When my friends asked me about eating off of her tray, I had my explanations lined up…I had watched her, she had not breathed on her French fries or touched them, therefore they were fair game. They should remember that in case she had food they wanted some day. Besides she had pretty eyes.

Over the course of the year, Beverly was one who was "just there" and I had to deal with. She wasn't mean, and she couldn't read so well, but it didn't matter. Beverly learned something important that I wasn't willing to learn. Beverly learned to make herself available when she had so little to give. She dealt with our cruel and deliberately vindictive behavior with aplomb. I selfishly learned to be protective of my interests and selective about how I spent my time and with whom. Even in the first grade, I realized, on some level, the truth is not always pretty, but it is present even if disguised like ketchup poured atop crunchy fries.

Billie

B- I –L- L- I- E. That was how he spelled his name. How would I know that? I made it my business to look at other peoples' papers at any opportune moment for two reasons. I wanted to see who made really pretty letters and who had to write the least amount of letters to make their name. (I was sure I had the most letters with M-a-r-g-a-r-e-t.) The opportunity came to check out other classmates' papers when I had to stand in the single file lines. It was best to get near the back of those lines so my curiosity could be sated (I got to see more papers), and I would not be as likely to get caught stepping out of line or, heaven forbid, talking. I discovered Billie's paper before I knew much about him. Billie's paper got noticed right away because his handwriting was so poor. His letters were all over the page.

Billie was a lean boy who looked like a miniature railroad workman, lacking only the cap and red bandana. (There must have been a rite of passage for boys from "The Hill" to wear striped bibbed overalls in the first grade, as they seemed to be the only students dressed that way.) However, Billie had something the other "Hill Boys" didn't have; he had an elevated shoe. This special shoe allowed him to stand with both feet hitting the ground at the same level, since his legs weren't the same length. When I think of his face, I remember Billie having large, brown eyes mixed with tiny flecks of gray. He appeared never to blink. Given the facts that his eyes were so vacant and he didn't talk much made him an immediate enigma. Billie also had very little hair on his head, just dark, closely cut follicles projecting from all points of his domed head. The most remarkable thing about Billie was the perpetual smile on his face. He had absolutely nothing whatsoever to smile about, yet he was constantly happy.

My classmates and I found out the most about each other on an almost "shade-less" sandlot in front of the school, the playground. Billie was so different from the rest of us. When someone threw a ball to him, he didn't know to catch it. The ball would bounce off his chest as if he was a rubberized human backboard. We tried to tell him to raise his arms to get, it but they just hung loosely from his shoulders, as if they didn't know what else to do. Occasionally he stumbled forward and staggered until he lost all sense of balance. When someone helped him get back on his feet, he smiled all the more, yet said so little. His discomposed nature began to spin an empathetic web that invisibly draped our class. When a group of us played house, Billie was often the little boy we had to take everywhere. Sometimes we "drove" him to the grocery store on a yellow wagon after we folded him up like a stackable toy. At other times we took turns lifting him up into an imaginary high chair or plopping him into a playpen. He grinned. He was easy to play with because he was a live doll we could arrange any way we wanted. Billie was fun to play with, unless he started drooling. Then he was left in the imaginary playpen only to be neglected by all of the mothers in the pretend houses.

In the classroom Billie couldn't learn to recite the alphabet phonetically every morning with the "ah, bu, cu, du, eh, fu, gu-s" the rest of us learned to recognize. No one laughed when he didn't know his colors or numbers, and someone at his table always helped him color. Billie couldn't hold one of those really fat pencils well either. Miss Smith looked after Billie and took him places from time to time. She sometimes came by and patted him on the back as if he had accomplished a great feat. Early in the year, she made it really clear that none of us was to mistreat Billie or tease him. We didn't.

It was not long into the school year when Billie had to leave. Our principal, my Aunt Ruth, came to the door one sunny fall morning with another lady. They came to get Billie. Miss Smith told us after he left that he wouldn't be back; he was going to a special school near Raleigh for mentally retarded students. He would live there and be taken care of by the state. Not totally understanding what it meant to be taken care of by the state, I knew something about that situation was disturbing.

I always wondered what happened to him and wondered if anybody ever cared about him since he had to leave his mama and daddy. Was he just left there to exist in dimly lit rooms with bare bulbs suspended from the ceiling? Did he sleep on a cot with a flimsy mattress made of ticking in a room that was never well lit? I pictured him existing in large darkened halls, sitting at bigger tables and being shocked with little rods if he or anyone else did something wrong. Did Billie learn to shuffle like a little prisoner through a soup line just to eat? My questions were never asked out loud. I never knew the answers. It bothered me in first grade that there were people in my class who had such problems that wouldn't go away. In the 1950's, before school integration, schools managed to educate some of us, but certainly not all of us. The "Billies" of the world lost out altogether. I wonder to what extent he knew the difference.

Epilogue

Years later I visited "Doodle Hill," knowing that life on "The Hill" has never been easy. I felt a foreign affection for the residents, lifelong survivors of numerous afflictions and poverty. Generations have been raised in this place, and some of the "Hillians" have become very respectable people. In this part of town, the yards dipped below street level and were not much more than shallow bowls of gray dirt with patches of wild grass tossed inside. Scattered about in the yards was anything from the past night's whiskey bottles, broken down stoves and washing machines, junked cars and tires to aging lawn furniture and yard art purchased on layaway. Many houses were not much more than dingy shingled cubes in disrepair. Front doors and side doors obviously opened into the same room. Back doors on such houses didn't exist. It was not uncommon to see homes with windows popped out and repaired with sheets of cardboard taped to window frames. Torn screens from porch doors and upstairs windows could be the only sign of domestic violence fueled by alcoholism or other forms of substance abuse. Life is hard on the hill. However, there is beauty on the hill as lovely old trees stately grace the perimeter of more pleasant yards trimmed with discount fencing. Pride appears in these modestly kept homes. Those who could afford to pay a minimum charge purchased children's riding toys, playhouses and inflatable swimming pools. Someone growing up in this environment with any wit surely learns to be inventive and savvy. Suffering is a way of life on the Hill; hope abounds in the three churches dotting the area. Broken families and dysfunctional living have not destroyed the spirits of some strong willed "Hillians." A sense of pride and confidence is reflected in the curtained windows, swept porches and sidewalks of the smattering of neatly kept residences. Which houses did my Doodle Hill classmates grow up in? I have no way of knowing.

Over the years I grew to admire my classmates who grew up on the Hill and bettered their lives. Beverly is now a registered nurse and no longer lives on the Hill. She has purchased a lovely home in town and maintains it well. Apparently, she continues to make herself available to others. I do not know what happened to Sammy or to Billie. The wise guy, Joel, who supplied my name to Sammy, did not live on the Hill. In my opinion, he befriended a "Hillian" for selfish motives, protection and entertainment. After high school, Joel graduated from the University of North Carolina as a John Motley Morehead Scholar and moved to Atlanta, Georgia.

Academics aside, in 1958 I learned simple life lessons in public school....life is not fair, life is not equal....life is the best we make it at any given moment. The more moments we take advantage of, the more successful we will be in terms of "getting our way." When people don't get their way, they become more unpredictable, often meaner. There are no easy solutions or formulas. Most six year olds learn this without prompting. Life repeats these lessons over and over and over again long after first grade. Miss Smith knew we would figure these lessons out without her tutelage.

4th of July Cookout

by D. S. Curtis

I was at the local Superstore, picking up hamburgers, buns, marshmallows, and all the necessaries for the day of our cookout. The family would be coming in, and there would be lots of eating, badminton, and around the clock Scrabble® games going on. We all looked forward to friends and family getting together and catching up on all the news. It is amazing to see how much those kids can grow in one year.

I was in charge of cleaning the house and making sure that there was a place for everyone to sleep. I purchased the food and prepared as much as possible ahead of time: baked beans, mac and cheese and deviled eggs are among the dishes to be served. My husband is in charge of the actual grilling and the campfire. The campfire is his specialty. We are not talking about your puny old candle sized campfire—we are talking bonfire size, the bigger the better—hotter than the sun and able to smelt steel. You know, the kind where you need to have 2 cleared acres and the bulldozer setting close by so that it's there if we need it. If we don't warn the fire department, we keep listening for sirens and looking for the fire engine to come around the corner any moment. NASA is sure to pick up our signal fire from space; our little glowing farm might even be pictured on their website one day. These are the thoughts I have while tossing lettuce, sodas and cheese in the grocery cart. I reassure myself that everything will be fine. It had been every year. Safely under the watchful control of my husband, who once a year becomes a pyromaniac. He is not alone in this love of fire either. All the guys contribute. I think fire is something that most men love to be able to control. I have to admit that I find it fascinating also. Fire is an act of nature that can be extremely destructive, completely unforgiving and unpredictable. Yet it is also purifying and illuminating. It reminds me of the "burning bush" that we all need to visit.

During the winter, our wood stove has to do. Fire in the sky in August from the Perseides meteor shower and Leonid meteor shower in November, but in July there is always the stack that we have worked to enlarge all year long. Some years it's bigger than others, but we have always tried to have the largest fire that we can manage.

As I leave the Superstore, I see they have the little fireworks tent section outside in the parking lot, men walking around the tent with their arms overflowing and their young son following closely behind. I have to smile. No last minute firework planning for my husband. He has been prepared for months.

Confessions of a Klutz

by Edward W. Allen

Bob Vila, Norm, and all of the other do-it-yourself crowd make it look so easy. And I'm sure everyone knows someone like my friend Mitch, a guy handy with tools who could single-handedly build a three bedroom house over the weekend and still have time to watch a game on TV—or rewire all of the electrical circuits in Yankee Stadium in an hour or so with time out for a coffee break—or...but why go on? You know what I mean. Some of us, however, are not quite so talented in that department. Let me be honest. I have trouble wrapping Christmas presents so you can imagine what I do with duct tape. When it comes to fixing things around the house, I am a bona fide, dyed-in-the-wool, card-carrying klutz. This sad fact, unfortunately, does not prevent my wife from finding opportunities for me to prove my ineptness over and over again. Well, as they say, love is blind. Or is it hope springs eternal? Let me give you an example.

We were in a huge Home Supply Center, one of those modern antiseptic hardware stores where everything comes in a shrink-wrapped container. We had come to purchase paint to redo the woodwork in the front bedroom. Somehow, we found ourselves passing through the plumbing department.

YOU CAN INSTALL THIS FAUCET YOURSELF! the container proclaimed in letters large enough to read from the parking lot. My wife stopped to examine the box in spite of my feeble efforts to urge her on. I knew only too well what that look on her face meant.

"We've got to do something about the kitchen faucet," she announced, "and there's no sense paying a plumber those high rates when we can do it ourselves."

I thought it best not to question exactly what she meant by *we*. As she finished her proclamation, we were approached by a kid who looked barely old enough to be able to ride a bicycle without training wheels. He wore the store's bright red blazer with a shiny name tag on the lapel that identified him as "Herbert."

"May I help you?" Herbert asked, flashing a toothy smile he had obviously been taught in training class. My wife questioned the veracity of the statement on the box.

"Oh, it's true," Herbert shot back almost before the last word left her mouth, "I put one in for my mother last week." Noting my look of disbelief, he added intensely, "Honest! I'll give you her phone number, and you can call and ask her."

My wife gave me a look, then turned to Herbert and made his day, "We'll take one."

Although she chose to ignore my uncontested ignorance regarding things mechanical, I agreed to do the job with the largess that has characterized husbands through the ages. I was thinking that, if this barely out-of-diapers kid could do it, there certainly was no reason I could not. That was my first mistake. I made the second mistake later at home. I started the job.

The first step was to remove the various cleaning materials and whatnot from under the sink. I wasn't being particularly careful because I assumed that, in this day and age, everything came in a spray can or a plastic bottle. I accidentally knocked one of the containers against that S-shaped pipe down there and discovered that it wasn't plastic. When it shattered, it spilled a thick, murky green liquid over the remaining cans and bottles, sending amoeba-like tendrils into the far corners of the cabinet. After that, it was all downhill. My wife's comments are best left unrecorded.

Cavalierly, I stepped aside so that she could clean up the mess. While she was so engaged, I read the directions for the installation of the faucet. "Disengage supply pipe nuts from faucet stems of old faucet. Loosen wing nuts and remove old faucet."

Quite honestly, I could not have understood it less if it had been written in Sanskrit. I hadn't a clue as to what a supply pipe was, let alone a supply pipe nut—or a faucet stem, for that matter. Still, I decided to press on. Otherwise, how would I be able to look Herbert in the eye again—assuming I ever went back there. After I got down on all fours to get started, it occurred to me that I would have to lie on my back and look upward in order to do whatever it was I was going to be doing down there. To do that, my bottom half would be on the kitchen floor, and my top half would be inside, under the sink, with the bottom of the cabinet opening across the middle of my back. This presented a slight problem. The bottom of the cabinet opening is some five inches higher than the floor, and I quickly learned that I do not bend that way. The solution was simple enough: a pillow from the bedroom. I admit, mine is on the old side—my wife cannot understand how someone can become attached to something as impersonal as a pillow, but, hey—and in some places, I'll admit, it is flattened with age and somewhat lumpy. So we used my wife's pillow.

Thus cushioned, I set to work. Using my unfailing sense of logic, I reasoned that the two copper tubes leading up to the underside of the old faucets were the supply pipes and, therefore, the supply pipe nuts must be those doodads at the top that attached them to the parts of the old faucets that stuck down under the sink, obviously the faucet stems. Sometimes, I amaze myself with my quick grasp of these technical details. A good thing I had thought to borrow a monkey wrench earlier from Vince, my next door neighbor, because I tried moving one of those nuts with my thumb and index finger. Let me put it this way. Arnold Schwarzenegger couldn't have budged it on his best day.

Though there was barely enough room to maneuver, I managed to get a grip with the wrench and turned. It took supreme effort, but it moved, and I was immediately drenched by a deluge of cold water spraying out all around the nut I had just loosened. I pushed with all my might, but could not turn the wrench back to retighten it enough to staunch the flow. My ever alert wife handed me a towel, which I felt was to wipe the water off my face. Instead, she told me to wrap it around the nut, which I did. The spray temporarily stopped, and I now had to contemplate my next move.

I again brought my mental abilities to the fore. Evidently, I thought, the object of being able to turn off a faucet is to prevent water from constantly flowing out of it. Therefore, before removing a faucet, I reasoned, it must be necessary to find some way to stop the water before it got up to the faucet. Brilliant! My wife pointed out the shut-off valves there under the sink at the bottom of what I had identified as the supply pipes. I turned them so that they stopped the water in its tracks. In doing so, I felt that I could possibly be in line for a Nobel award.

The water now stopped, I had to go and change my shirt before getting back to work—also had to get another pillow, as my wife's was now water-logged—not my pillow, though—maybe one from the spare bedroom. While I was changing, my wife used a couple of bath towels and half a roll of paper towels to wipe up the puddles under the sink.

Once more, I bent to the task. Or, rather, laid down to it. This time, without the water to hamper me, I was able to loosen one nut completely. The other was a bit more difficult. The more I strained, the more I perspired. The more I perspired, the more my bifocals slid down my nose, so that I was being forced to try to see through the wrong lens or past the frames. Nothing was clear. Finally, in frustration, I took them off, figuring I could see better without them, and laid them outside the cabinet on the kitchen floor, beside my waist, where I could reach them if I needed them.

I don't know if you have ever had an opportunity to study the under side of your kitchen sink, but let me tell you, it's a whole other world under there—all kinds of junk—glop, gunk, residue, rust, stuff like that. I mention rust because me banging around with the monkey wrench dislodged some rust that floated with unerring accuracy down into my now unprotected eyes. It felt like I had a mountain of sharp rocks under each eyelid. In my mind's eye, I could envision enlargements of minute chunks of jagged rusted metal doing horrendous things to my eyeballs. In a matter of milliseconds, I reasoned that I should go to the bathroom to rinse them out. In scrambling out from under the sink, I forgot about my glasses and zigged when I should have zagged. I landed right on top of them and broke the frame and cracked one of the lenses. At that moment, however, the pain in my eyes held center stage. It occurred to me, on the way to the bathroom, that flushing the grit out was the way to go. Summoning my willpower to heroic proportions, with my eyes closed, I took the time to adjust the hot and cold faucets, get the rubber syringe out of the medicine cabinet and fill it with lukewarm water.

I pulled each eyelid forward and squirted under each in turn. Almost instantly, a searing fire ignited both eyes, and I felt compelled to react from the depths of my soul. Vince and Stella told us later that they didn't know whether to call the police or an ambulance. They decided to wait and see because they had heard me singing in the shower once and thought I might be holding forth again. When my wife reached the bathroom, she found me sitting on the floor, propped against the tub with the shower curtain that I had managed to pull down draped around my shoulders and my hands clasped to my eyes. She soaked cotton balls in mineral oil, laid them on my eyes, and wrapped a gauze bandage around my head.

When we got back from the hospital emergency room, I could see somewhat, and the pain had subsided a little. Evidently, according to the doctor, in flushing the rust out of my eyes, I had inadvertently also flushed out the eyes' natural lubricant so that the raw inner surfaces of the eyelids were in direct contact with the raw outer surfaces of the eyeballs. There was some good news, though. I wasn't going to be able to see well enough to help my wife paint the woodwork in the front bedroom.

While I took to my bed to convalesce, my wife finished installing the new faucet in the kitchen—took her about fifteen minutes. As I lay there, I mentally totaled up what the faucet had cost. First, there was the $59.95 plus tax that we paid for the faucet at Herbert's store. The trip to the emergency room cost $135. Another $11.95 went to the pharmacy for special eye drops. A new frame and a lens for my glasses cost $92, and it took $15 to replace the torn shower curtain. And it would cost another $10.68 (tax included) to replace the cleaning liquid—that murky green stuff— that had spilled under the sink. And finally, $20 for a new pillow for my wife, plus…well, it just wasn't pretty. But look at it from my wife's point of view. At least we didn't have to call a plumber and pay him $65 for a half hour's work.

After the Harvest

by Mabel Janet Wood

In the 1960's, during a typical hot summer evening, our family could be found at my grandmother's house harvesting the multitude of vegetables that had been carefully planted earlier in the season. Rarely were there less than eight adults and nine children at this yielding.

The two-story, wood-frame house was painted bright white. There was a spacious front porch and a creaky wooden back porch that extended the width of the house. Approximately seven to ten wooden steps ascended on either side. The long back porch was where the women sat to prepare the food for canning and freezing.

Around the house was grass that looked like a big green carpet and cascaded down by the back of the house under the sagging weeping willow tree. There were towering oak trees on either side of the yard that mirrored guards standing at a gate.

In the one-acre garden, there were strong green stalks of corn that stood at attention like soldiers waiting for inspection. On these sturdy stalks were two to four ears of sweet white or yellow corn, wrapped in light green husks that were wrinkled like party crepe paper. At the top of the closed husk, you could see thick strands of silk that was a light blond color. It deepened to a dark brown, coarser silk closer to the husks. The taste of this tender corn was milky sweet!

Next to the corn were delicate green vines growing close to the ground like garland wrapping a Christmas tree. The sweet peas that the vines gave resembled dark green pearls boxed in a lighter green shell. From another green vine, we harvested fresh yellow squash in varying sizes and shapes. Some of them appeared to be instruments used to make music at a Mexican fiesta. The juicy, red tomatoes were the size of baseballs.

Once washed and dried, the rich deep color was brilliant red. The veins on the inside appeared to be tiny roads extending in all directions, while the small yellow seeds represented houses stationed on either side.

To one side of the backyard, one could find scratchy brown burlap bags in which the corn was brought from the garden. Handled buckets in round and square shapes were used for transporting the delicious tomatoes, squash and peas. The silver or white colors had tiny rust spots, where the water had eaten away at the paint.

Gone are the days after the harvest! Gone, too, are many of the harvesters. The garden is now someone else's green back yard. The weeping willow no longer uses its long sagging branches to sweep the carpeted ground. There are no more exciting stories of trips to the cannery. The old wooden two-story house is still white, but different family stories reside inside and out.

You Don't See Me!

by Ruthann P. Anderson

The first week of August had just come to a close. Because of the heat, John and I postponed our afternoon walk in the woods until the early evening hours when the temperature was cooler and less humid. This had been an exceptionally hot, dry summer. The severe drought of the past few years continued with no relief in sight.

On this particular evening, John and I and our dog Molly had completed three-quarters of our walk and had just passed Lookout Rock. Molly was somewhere ahead of us, as usual. When we caught up with her, she was on full alert at the base of a large red cedar tree near the edge of the woods. We knew from her body language that something was there. She didn't bark, growl or jump, but her eyes were fixed on something in the tree. Molly frequently sees and hears things that John and I don't, but we always investigate each situation. Our eyes slowly scanned the tree trunk upward from its base. Ten feet above the ground and clinging to the trunk of the tree was a dark brown furry animal; it was a groundhog, also known as a woodchuck.

John and I are very familiar with woodchucks scurrying across the field and disappearing into large round holes in the ground in the immediate vicinity. Although they are good climbers, we had never before had any high-rise sightings. We assumed Molly was bouncing along through the field of clover when the woodchuck heard her coming or picked up her scent. He must not have had time to return to his den.

For me, any wildlife encounter transforms an ordinary day into a special one. I slowly and quietly walked around the cedar to get a better look at the groundhog from all angles. The woodchuck turned his head in slow motion in my direction; he scrutinized every move I made. John and Molly remained in front of the tree while I continued to study our friend from different vantage points. I felt sorry for the furry creature; he looked so frightened, not knowing what we were going to do to him. I spoke calmly to try to reassure him that we meant no harm. The groundhog's small dark brown eyes continued to reflect his inner fear. I could only imagine what he was thinking:

What are you looking at lady? You don't see me. I'm just a shadow on the tree trunk. I know what you humans do to critters like me. Humans don't have a very good reputation amongst us woodland creatures. You point those noisy *sticks* at us, and then *boom*! We never see our friends and family again. What did we ever do to you? Okay, maybe we nibbled a few plants; we were just trying to get a bite to eat. Don't you eat when you are hungry? I'll be happy to go back to my comfortable den if you would kindly leave. Be sure to take that big black bouncy thing with you!

John, Molly and I continued to watch the groundhog. He remained perfectly motionless, except to turn his head ever so slowly as we moved slightly one way or the other. I still felt sorry for this frightened animal and had no intentions of hurting him. He even seemed to tug a little on John's heartstrings, a major accomplishment for any groundhog! Woodchucks are *not* on John's favorite animals list!

John and I continued our journey back to the house. Molly raced past us and ran up ahead. Her ears bounced up and down with each footstep. If her ears were attached with hinges, the hinges would be worn out by now! Her waggy tail temporarily disappeared from view. There were so many other scents to investigate and things to see. By the time John and I arrived back at the house, Molly was there waiting for us. She looked at us as if to ask, "What took you so long?" We suspect the groundhog was now in the safety of his den, hoping never to see the three of us again!

ABOUT THE AUTHORS

Edward W. Allen

After service in the United States Marine Corps in WWII and Korea, Ed, who turned 81 years of age in September of 2006, worked the graveyard shift for six years while attending the University of Pittsburgh, where he received his Bachelor's and Master's degrees. He began working towards his doctorate at Columbia University while teaching high school and as an Assistant Professor at a state college. He left academia to enter the business world and spent the next 32 years as a Training and Human Resource Development Consultant. In that capacity, he wrote textbooks and created numerous training programs for a number of firms in business, industry, government, and the military, including General Aniline & Film, Paine Webber, AT&T, Sunoco, Phelps Dodge, U.S. Army, U.S. Navy, U.S. Department of State, and the U.S. Department of Health, Education, and Welfare. He retired as Vice President and Director of Educational Services for a national trade association headquartered in New York. He met his wife, JoAnn, in 1953 and proposed to her on their second date. They have two sons, Robert and Thomas, and celebrated their 52nd anniversary in September, 2006. Following retirement, he and JoAnn, a retired Registered Nurse, purchased a 100 acre farm in Red Oak, Virginia. With the help of their son Tom, who lived nearby, they completely renovated and modernized a dilapidated antebellum manor house and operated a vacation farm for six years. They recently sold the farm and moved into a smaller house where he continues with his writing. He explains, "Sitting in a rocking chair on the porch and watching grass grow is not retirement. It's boring." And, as a friend said, "It's stagnation."

Ruthann P. Anderson

Ruthann P. Anderson received both her B.S. and M.S.Ed. degrees from the State University of New York at Plattsburgh. Her first experience as a writer came while working on her college newspaper. Since then, she has written a variety of things, some of which have been published. In addition to writing, Mrs. Anderson is an animal lover. She has taken in orphaned and injured animals since early childhood, helping those she could and turning others over to proper authorities. She is also an experienced seamstress, embroiderer, crafter and quilter. She also enjoys cooking and baking.

Kristi Tuck Austin

Kristi Tuck Austin grew up in Virgilina, Virginia. Encouraged by her family, she began writing at a young age. She wrote for high school publications and went on to graduate from the University of Virginia in 2005 with degrees in English literature and religious studies. She and her husband Adam currently reside in Richmond while she completes her master's degree.

Sylvia Carey

Sylvia Carey wrote her first play while studying at Trinity University in San Antonio, Texas. The play was performed by the Trinity University Players, and the writing bug was born. Later she received a Masters Degree in Reading from Indiana University. She started the first Volunteer Reading Program for adults in Halifax County while working for Longwood College. Annually she attends the Nimrod Hall Summer Arts Program for writers in Goshen, Virginia. She is married, lives in Halifax County, has five children and thirteen grandchildren. "NASCAR Phantom" is a story written to inspire everyone to follow their dreams.

Andy Coe

Like most poets, Andy started dabbling with the art form as a way to impress "chicks." Most of his work from that period was awful and, therefore, ineffective. (In retrospect he wishes he would have picked up the guitar.) Fortunately, most of it had been lost or destroyed before he met his wife. After a 20 year hiatus from poetry, in which—among other things—he got married, got a real job, and had five children, he has gotten back into it, but for very different reasons—namely as a way of making friends with the mysteries of life as he meets them.

Don Conner

Don Conner was a teacher of English for many years. He taught in local schools before retiring in 1998. In the 1970's and 1980's, he served separate tenures as editor of two literary journals: *The Piedmont Literary Review* and *Proof Rock*.

Margaret Covington

Margaret Covington is a native North Carolinian. As a middle child, she learned to use a vivid imagination to make sense of the world. "There was always this energy in our family that was tireless at times. As a family of talkers, we were encouraged to be literate and informed," she says. "Writing became a way of expressing myself and exploring my thoughts while in elementary school. I wanted to be a writer in fifth grade." Margaret, a teacher in Halifax County Public Schools, resides in Halifax, VA with her husband, Bill. They have two children, Katherine and Ned.

D. S. Curtis

D. S. Curtis is an international traveler, an avid reader and hails from a literary family. She enjoys gardening, carpentry, needlecrafts, raising poultry, painting and sketching. She is an editor, a freelance columnist, a Public Relations specialist for the Woman of Hope, a Master Gardener, an independent *Bible* scholar and a co-author of a study guide for the book of *Revelation*. She is currently working on a novel and editing several manuscripts. She resides with her husband and daughter in Southside Virginia.

Gene Curtis

Gene Curtis is the author of the acclaimed novel *The Seventh Mountain*. A retired police sergeant, his close attention to detail brings his settings, scenes, and characters to life. The author of many short stories, he weaves masterfully intricate plots, incorporating the entire spectrum of human emotion, leaving his readers eagerly anticipating more. He is a member of the Science Fiction Writers critique group *Critters*, and the esteemed *Writers Studio* of South Central Virginia where he currently resides with his wife and daughter.

Melissa Elmes

A native of Williamsburg, Virginia and a graduate of the college of William and Mary, Melissa Elmes pretends to be a professional high-school English/Art History teacher while pursuing her true vocation as a starving artist. A writer, actor, singer, dancer, and artist by nature and inclination, she shares her word-heavy world with her husband, daughter, three dogs and a cat. Her work includes fiction, poetry, academic articles, news and editorial pieces, song lyrics, personal essay/memoir and...a blog (although she still doesn't believe her husband when he tells her so.) She has been published in the **Blotter**, the **Gazette-Virginian**, and two poetry anthologies.

Michele Marko Fitch

Michele Marko Fitch was born and raised in Pittsburgh, PA, but now lives in South Boston, Virginia with her husband, Ron, and three-year-old daughter, Kathryn. She is the proud stepmother to Meagan, who also has an interest in writing. Mrs. Fitch is a graduate of Slippery Rock University and Longwood College. She is a former educator of students with special needs. She developed an early love of literature from her mother and grandmother. Her grandmother was a published author of several children's stories. She enjoys reading, water skiing, swimming, singing, cross-stitch, sewing and other crafts.

S. M. Foran

Originally from the western United States, S.M. Foran earned a Bachelor of Arts in English in 1994 and a Master of Arts in English in 1996. He has had a number of poems and short stories published and is currently working on a novel, **Woundward Flight of the Ancient Young**. He now teaches writing and literature in Virginia, where he lives with his wife, Kimberly.

Wayne D. Hodge

Wayne Hodge is a native of Halifax County in Virginia. He was educated in the local public schools of Halifax County. He is a veteran of the United States Navy and served on the USS CONNOLE during his tour of duty. He is presently residing in Halifax County. "Wolfbane Blues" is the first published work of this author. Wayne is currently working on a series of short stories.

Susan Hall Jernigan

Susan is a full time nursing student working on her RN degree. Her hobbies include crocheting, reading, listening to music, writing, and anything to do with the Civil War. She is employed part time at Sentara Obici Hospital as a Monitor/EKG Technician. She has two grown sons who reside in North Carolina. She resides in Suffolk, VA with her husband and three young daughters.

Eva Lacks

Active member U.M.C., certified lay speaker, mission trip Mexico City, soloist, songwriter. Gospel recording artist, artist, watercolor and acrylics, interior design consultant, decorating with antiques, voracious reader. Laughingly admits two or three fiction stories are in the computer at all times, somewhat, like "Changing Hats." Currently working on some material for submission to Noble Publishing, UK. Published by World of Poetry: "His Love." Published by Sparrowgrass Forum: "Her Calmness." Honorable mention awards, "No Time to Stop," "Dare to Dream," "Reflections." "Love" to be published in Immortal Voices. Favorite pastime, visiting art museums and galleries. Loves to travel in search of Victorian/country antiques. Resides with her husband, J.A., at "Windhaven Farm." She chose *AVE el* as her signature.

Martha H. Lester

Martha H. Lester, a native of Halifax County, VA , and a retired licensed nurse of 27 years active duty nursing, graduated from Halifax County public schools and Halifax

Regional Hospital's School of Practical Nursing. She attended Averett Junior College, Danville, VA, for a certificate in Secretarial Science. She holds an Associate of Arts in General Studies from Charter Oaks State College in New Britain, Connecticut. Her hobbies include fictional writing, hymn writing, poetry, drawing poster Artz-4-Kidz, reading and music. She serves actively at First Baptist Church of North Main Street in South Boston, as a teen's class Sunday School teacher, a member of the Diaconate Board, and the Chancel Choir. She resides in South Boston, VA.

Shirley A. Mandel

Shirley A. Mandel is a Christian poet who has overcome a disability to acquire a college education. She did undergraduate work at Averett University and graduated with two B.A. degrees, one in English and one in journalism. She has also won several awards at Averett for excellence in poetry. Born in Baltimore, she trained as an x-ray-technician earlier in her life, and she did a stint in the Army at the end of the Vietnam War. She served in a Vietnamese refugee camp as a medical soldier, which was one of her earlier life dreams. Currently she is working as a volunteer at Good Samaritan Ministries, a ministry to the poor in the community. She likes to help people.

H. T. Owen

H.T. Owen is a retired teacher. She lives on a farm where she says the quiet, peaceful setting is conducive to writing. She is the author of several published stories, poems, and articles. She and her husband have three adult sons who have often been an inspiration for her writing. H.T. Owen says, "I have always loved words, and I declared at a very early age that I would become an *authoress*."

Doris Ragland

Ms. Ragland is a graduate of Halifax County Training School, Halifax, Virginia. She is also a graduate of North Carolina College at Durham, North Carolina with a Bachelor's degree in Home Economics. Ms. Ragland is a graduate of Teacher's College, Columbia

University, New York with a Master's degree in Family Life Education. Her publishing history includes poems, articles, and editorials published in *The Carolina Peacemaker Weekly News*, *The Baptist Informer* (a publication o0f the General Baptist State Convention of Raleigh, NC), *The North Carolina Teacher's Record Magazine*, and *The Lott Carey Foreign Mission Convention Magazine* of Washington, D.C.

Barbara Hatcher Shaver

Barbara Hatcher Shaver is a native of Halifax County. Currently she lives in Danville with her husband, Jerry. They have two children and three grandchildren. She is a Magna Cum Laude graduate of Virginia Commonwealth University with a Bachelor of Interdisciplinary Studies degree in Creative Writing and Human Services. She was awarded a diploma in Writing for Children and Teenagers from the Institute of Children's Literature. Her publishing credits include writing for a college newspaper and winning a newspaper contest. A devotion of hers will be published by the Virginia Conference Children's Initiative Committee in their 2007 Lenten Devotional.

Lillian K. Stumm

Lillian K. Stumm (1914-1998) published the following children's stories: *The Mouse Who Wanted the Moon*, *Wake Up Rooster*, and *Upsy Daisy*. The Starlets recorded her song, "Mouse in the House." She left many other children's stories and songs. Some were complete. Others, including "Jolly Mr. Holly," were unfinished. She was married to Edward L. and had two children, Sylvia and Edward F., and five grandchildren, including Michele Marko Fitch. She was a graduate of Slippery Rock Normal School and taught elementary school. She enjoyed reading, playing Scrabble, playing sports, singing, and playing the piano and violin.

Sarah Tuck

Sarah Tuck attended public schools in Halifax County through the tenth grade then boarded at St. Mary's Junior College for four years. This school emphasized liberal arts and handwriting skills and an interest in literature. After receiving an associate of arts degree, she attended the University of Tennessee, where she majored in French and minored in English. She taught English at the local high school and became a social worker a few years later. A windfall in writing came when Mrs. Tuck accepted a post at the local **News and Record** to be a feature writer and photographer. Stories were everywhere, waiting to be written. A few years later she, became a clerk in the library. She was exposed again to good writing and creative ideas.

Mabel Janet Wood

Mabel Janet Wood (Janet, as her friends and family call her) became disabled in 1998 and since that time has been proactive in her health management of Fibromyalgia Syndrome. She became a volunteer with the National Fibromyalgia Association to spread awareness of this chronic illness that affects millions of adults and some children. Along with volunteering, Janet sings soprano in her church gospel choir, takes photographs, makes jewelry and writes poetry. She was nominated as a *2006 Poetry Ambassador* earlier this year and in October was nominated for *Who's Who in Poetry* by the International Library of Poetry.

**For more information on the Writers Studio,
please email us at: inkwrit@yahoo.com,
or visit our website: website:
*http://members.gcronline.com/writersstudio/***

www.ingramcontent.com/pod-product-compliance
Lightning Source LLC
Chambersburg PA
CBHW030139180626
46812CB00002B/767